Italian Sunsets

Luna Family Trilogy

Kimberly R. Rose

Published by Kimberly R. Rose, 2023.

Table of Contents

To my sisters, who have always encouraged me and believed in me. I couldn't have done this without either of you.

Prologue

Natala Luna tried to ignore her wet cheeks as she sat in the dark, running her fingers over the cover of a worn notebook. The notebook was smaller than her school notebooks had been, more of a journal. The cover was pink with a picture of the Eiffel tower on the front.

Natala tried not to think about how much her heart hurt, choosing to focus on the notebook instead. She hadn't seen it for years; it had been hiding on a shelf in her closet.

Natala had gotten it as a child, and now the inside was full of the places she wanted to visit all over France. When she'd begun French classes in high school, she'd tried to start writing vocabulary in the back of the notebook. She'd failed that class, so there was no telling how accurate the vocabulary section was.

When she heard the apartment door open, Natala jumped in surprise before wiping the tears off her face. Her roommate wasn't supposed to be home this early, it was still morning. Wasn't it? She blinked at the bright light that the girl turned on. "Natala? What are you doing here?" Kate asked. "Honey, what's wrong?" Kate noticed the tears Natala couldn't quite wipe away, and the swollen eyes that indicated she'd been crying for a while.

Kate ran over to Natala, feeling an urge to comfort her. She hugged her tightly. "You were supposed to be with-"

"Don't even say it." Natala let her notebook fall on the floor and felt her eyes well up with tears yet again as her heart filled with pain. "I don't want to hear his name."

Frowning, Kate tried to look Natala in the eyes, something Natala avoided by closing hers. "Natala..." She trailed off. *What was she supposed to say?* Crying wasn't characteristic of Natala. In fact, Kate wasn't sure she'd ever seen her roommate cry before.

Natala grabbed the blanket she had thrown on the floor earlier and used it to bury herself on the couch. Kate shrugged; Natala would tell

1

her more when she was ready. She stood up and picked up some bags. "I brought leftovers." Kate said softly. "I'm going to put some on a plate for you and heat it up. I'm not sure what you need right now, but my nonna taught me there is nothing that can't be solved with food."

"Ice cream." Natala muttered softly from under her blanket, her voice rough from all the crying she'd done. "Nothing else sounds good." She hugged the fluffiness of the blanket closer to her, as if that would take the pain away or make her tears stop.

Kate ignored her dramatics and put a plate full of food in the microwave, then walked over to the couch. She picked up the notebook that Natala had been looking at earlier. "What is this?" She asked her as she opened it and noted the sketches of the Eiffel tower and Louvre Museum.

"Nothing." Natala replied, slowly peeking her head out from the blanket. "Just all my childhood dreams for my honeymoon. I had it all planned out. Destinations - how much they would cost, how long it would take to travel from place to place, all the logistics. French words that may..." Sniffles interrupted her words, "Or may not be correct." She disappeared back into the blankets at the same time the microwave beeped.

Kate carried the notebook over to the kitchen and set it by the sink, then pulled the food out of the microwave and set it down on the table. Flipping to another page in the notebook, she opened a drawer and pulled out silverware. "Your dinner is ready." She told Natala, then filled the tea kettle and put that on the stove.

Natala didn't want to leave her blanket, something about it was safe and comforting. Her heart was the only thing that had been broken, but her whole body felt like it hurt. Before too long, the smell of the food Kate had heated won. Natala carefully climbed out of her blanket, trying not to get caught in it or trip. She walked over to the table and sat down as Kate did the same, a mug of tea in her hand.

"Merry Christmas." She told her roommate sarcastically before she dug into the lasagna. Her sarcasm came out more when she felt strong emotions – no matter what those emotions were.

"Happy Birthday!" Kate smiled. "I brought you a piece of chocolate cake that my mama insists she made, though I think she actually got it from Walmart yesterday." Kate raised her eyebrows as she watched Natala eat. "It's like 6pm Natala, have you eaten anything today? How long have you been sitting in the dark?"

"Some birthday." Natala mumbled through the food. She continued to eat, ignoring Kate's questions. As soon as Natala ate the final bite on her plate, Kate jumped up and took a plastic container out of a bag. She opened a cupboard door and rummaged through it. "I'm sure we have candles somewhere." She said to herself.

"Junk drawer." Natala reminded her as she stood up and rinsed off the plate, then set the silverware on top of the plate in the sink. She carefully took two plates out of the cupboard and set each on the table, along with a fork.

Kate emerged from the junk drawer with the candles and noted the plates with a frown. "This is your cake. One plate."

Natala met her eyes for the first time that day - Christmas day. "I'm not eating cake alone on my birthday." Her voice cracked on the last word, and a tear slipped down her cheek as she sat back down on her chair.

Kate bit her lip, then shook her head as if she'd decided against arguing and sat down. She cut the slice of cake in half and put a slice on each of the plates, then added a green candle to Natala's slice of cake. She lit the candle. "Happy Birthday to you, Happy-"

Her off-pitch singing was cut off abruptly as Natala blew out the candle with a woosh of air that seemed excessive, then pulled the candle out of the cake and added it to Kate's plate.

"Yeah, okay." Kate picked up her fork and took a bit of the cake, then smiled. "I don't care if this is a Walmart cake, it's a chocolate cake.

Chocolate cake is always delicious." She eyed Natala, who was silently eating her cake. "And chocolate is your favorite. You have to tell me something Natala. Your eyes are red and I am worried about you. You were supposed to be gone until tomorrow."

"I don't know how long I've been here." Natala took another bite of her cake and sighed. "I'm twenty-five, Kate. Twenty-five." The cake felt good going down her sore throat. She'd never realized how much crying could irritate her throat, but she'd also never had a reason to cry this much.

"It's your golden birthday!" Kate's eyes widened as she realized what she'd just pointed out. "I should have gotten you something gold. A gold candle at least."

"I'm glad you didn't." Natala looked down at her cake. "I always thought I'd be married by now. I'd be happy, I'd have a great job, start a family before too long-" She sighed again.

"Is this about Nolen?" Kate asked. "Did you want him to propose?"

Natala snorted. "Want him to? Want him to? I *expected* him to. We'd talked about it many times over this year, how he was finally ready. It was - or is, I guess - my golden birthday. It's also Christmas and it was the perfect day. I thought there was a plan there, thought I'd be getting a ring and planning my wedding." She stabbed her fork back onto her cake, the end of it hitting the plate hard enough to make Kate flinch.

"That didn't happen?" Kae asked, figuring she knew the answer already. No one acted like this after they'd had their dreams come true.

"I got a tennis bracelet." Natala lifted her eyebrows and looked at Kate again. "He gave me a tennis bracelet. Said it was gold for my golden birthday, and I didn't know what to say. So, I excused myself to go to the bathroom. I thought maybe he was waiting until later, like he wanted it to be a special moment between the two of us. But then he said that he had had a talk with his parent's last week, and they had helped him realize that we weren't ready yet for something as big as marriage."

A sob came from Natala, and she used her hands to cover her face. 'He said that we weren't ready for marriage. I asked him when he would be ready." She shook her head. "He told me that he wasn't sure. He's a lawyer climbing the ranks at his dad's company and I just work in a factory."

Kate's jaw dropped. She knew well that Natala didn't love her factory job. Natala simply tolerated it, but she stayed because it paid twice what she could get anywhere else. Her parents had no extra money to help her for college, she hadn't qualified for scholarships, and she thought going into debt would be unwise. So, she started working at the factory - putting bottles into boxes and quality checking - at seventeen. Now she paid all her bills and was still able to put something into savings each month.

It was something that Natala had told Kate many times she was proud of, how hard she had worked and how well she had used the money she had, or more accurately, hadn't used. She'd hoped to buy a house soon after getting married.

Natala broke the silence. "I told him it was over. If he wasn't ready after ten flipping years of dating then it wasn't going to happen." She started to cough, as if she had run out of air. "Here." Kate pushed a glass of water into her hands, watching her carefully.

Natala took a sip of water, then placed the cup back onto the table. "So here I am, twenty-five and single for the first time in my adult life. With a factory job and no college degree. On Christmas, of all the days."

Kate was quiet, her eyes returning to the notebook that Natala had thrown earlier. "I have an idea." She said slowly.

Natala frowned. "What?" She asked. "I'm not going out and getting drunk." She'd heard that alcohol would numb the pain, but hopefully time would have the same effect. She had gotten drunk once in her life and had promptly decided that would be the last time.

Kate laughed. "That was one time. I promised it wouldn't happen again." She pointed to the notebook. "Doesn't the factory close for those two weeks every May? You are a strong, independent woman, maybe it's time for you to take life into your own hands and go on a trip."

Natala blinked; the thought had never occurred to her.

She usually spent those two weeks with Nolen's mother, helping her with various tasks and learning to cook. Practice for her own home, she'd always thought. That wouldn't be happening this year. "It can be my birthday and Christmas present to myself." She said with a smile as the Christmas lights in the center of the table made her eyes sparkle. "It's about time I did something for myself."

Chapter 1

That was how Natala found herself standing at the airport five months later, trying to find her gate. The nerves were there in full force, but her adventure was just beginning. She was ready to get away from home. It had been a boring and lonely five months, as Natala realized she really didn't know many people in her city or even in the state. She'd moved from Wisconsin to Illinois when she was eighteen, following her ex to college. Other than her coworkers, she'd known no one but Kate and Nolen. Her heartbreak had lasted a couple months, then it had given way to indifference as Natala anticipated this adventure.

Natala had originally wanted to go to Paris as she had planned all those years ago, wanted to visit the Eiffel tower and sample the pastries she could almost smell from all the descriptions she wrote. She'd studied her sketches and tried to imagine being in France. But it hadn't seemed right. Every time she had tried to plan her trip there had been a stab of pain that she was going by herself.

Kate had been the one to suggest Italy, because her great-grandparents had immigrated from there and she'd grown up hearing her grandmother's stories about growing up in the country. She promised Natala that Italy has pastries just as good as French pastries, along with pasta and enough cheese to make her mouth water. That's when Natala had shrugged her agreement. Kate had gone into planning mode, saying she knew exactly where and what Natala should visit. Natala was flying in to Rome, but she would be visiting different cities throughout her trip.

Her Eiffel tower notebook was back in her apartment, and she was armed with a new notebook now. Plain blue, Kate had purchased it for her and had been the one to write down her itinerary. She was taking a weeklong trip, and Kate had planned one activity for her each day. Kate had said that way, she had a plan and would get out at least once each day, but she encouraged Natala to explore the country for herself as well. That wasn't Natala's strong suit, she liked her plans. Like the engagement plan, that one had gone so well for her.

As she prepared and packed, Natala learned that it wasn't just on vacation there were expenses. The passport had been an expense as well. And in the process, she had gone to the courthouse in her city to apply for one only to find out she was missing her birth certificate.

Her mother still had it apparently. Her mom had dug through the paperwork that crowded her small office in the house Natala had grown up in, then had mailed the document to Natala.

That time Natala had been able to successfully submit her application, and it had taken nine long weeks to get to her.

Natala paused her reminiscing and felt her pocket, making sure the passport was still there. She was terrified of losing it, terrified about anything that could go wrong on this trip. Some days leading up to this one she had thought about canceling. But it has been way too long since she'd done something for herself. Her plans had always been made with her ex in mind, or made around what her ex planned for them to do.

"There it is." Natala whispered to herself as she found her gate. She sat down in a chair as soon as she could find one, then began to look around the crowded airport. Natala had flown maybe twice in her life, and that was back when she was a child. Her parents used to take her and her siblings on vacations in the States. This was the first vacation Natala was taking since then.

She smiled as she heard the accents of people around her. She had always found accents fascinating. Working in the factory, they had many different people come from different states for the summer. These were more than just American accents though, many of them seemed to be Italian, which made sense when one was flying to Italy. She heard many other accents she couldn't place as people spoke and walked around her.

"Hello." An elderly lady greeted Natala. "Do you mind if I sit?"

Natala immediately moved her bag to the floor. "Not at all, I'm sorry my things were in your way."

"Thank you my dear." The lady sat down slowly, leaning on her cane for assistance. "These bones just aren't what they used to be. I used to go skydiving you know, back in the day."

"Skydiving?" Natala looked at her a bit closer. At 5' 2", Natala was shorter than many people she knew; but this lady was shorter than she was. Skinny too, which could have been mistaken for frail if one didn't notice the sparkle of life and mischief in her eyes.

"Oh yes, my dear, skydiving. It was a great thrill, to jump from a plane into the unknown. Of course, it wasn't exactly unknown and the pilot always made sure it was a safe place for us to jump. But when you can barely see the ground, it felt like a jump into a mystery land." The lady patted Natala's hand. "Life is too short to stay on the ground. One must get out of the rut life has made for us and go jump into something new. It makes you a stronger person."

Natala pondered this as the lady opened her bag and pulled out a pillow, apparently intending to take a nap while they awaited time to board. Was this trip - this jump into the unknown - going to make her a stronger person?

Natala looked around the airport, then let herself sink back into the reminiscing. The past couple months had seemed make her a stronger person, as Natala learned how to be single.

As a teenager she hadn't thought about the fact that she was single, she'd just been happy with her friends and enjoying school. It had been normal, as much as something could be normal. When Nolen came along it had seemed so perfect, so natural to begin dating him. She'd only been fifteen at that point. What did a fifteen-year-old know about lasting love?

Then ten years had gone by and they'd both grown up, grown together. "At least that's what I thought." Natala whispered aloud, a quick flash of pain surprising her. Apparently, Nolen had had other ideas. After ten years he still wasn't sure he wanted to spend the rest of his life with her.

Natala looked down at her finger and shook herself out of her thoughts. When her coworker Mandy had found out about the unfortunate event, she'd insisted on taking her ring shopping. Natala hadn't been keen on the idea at first. Why was a single girl going ring shopping? But Mandy had apparently known what she was doing when they went to an antique store. Natala had found a beautiful jade ring; one she now wore every day. It reminded her that she was strong all on her own; and it didn't hurt that the ring was pretty.

"Boarding group C in five minutes." Came over the loudspeaker. Natala fumbled for her ticket before she checked her group.

"Group C." She said, not realizing the smile that came over her face. "Here we go."

***

An hour later, Natala had boarded the plane and found her seat. She didn't remember anything about the takeoff process from her family trips. Her hands felt like they were shaking, but she ignored the urge to check. Instead, she looked out the window of the plane and wondered why she hadn't taken a short flight in the States to prepare.

"Good afternoon." A man stowed a bag into the bin above Natala, then sat down in the seat next to her. "It looks like we are neighbors for the flight. Seatmates, whatever term you prefer." He winked at her as he sat down.

Natala smiled at the man, wondering where he was from. She couldn't place the accent; it sounded like it had come from more than one part of the world. "Looks like it." She replied, then pulled a book out of her backpack. Reading had always calmed her nerves, maybe she could distract herself from the takeoff.

"Introduction to Italy." The man grinned as he read the title of Natala's book. "Your first time visiting?"

Natala looked up. "Yes." She replied, not entirely sure if she wanted to have a conversation with this man. How did she know he wasn't a scammer or something? That he wasn't going to kidnap her? *My nerves may be turning into paranoia,* she admitted to herself.

"Tony Calo." The man held out his hand.

Natala cautiously shook his hand. "Natala." She left her last name out, figuring one couldn't be too safe. "Have you been to Italy before?"

Tony chuckled as he gestured to the bag sitting on his lap. "You could say that. I've been to many places before, many times. Freelance photographer, I specialize in international photography. Don't tell my clients, but Italy is my personal favorite. It's where my madre grew up."

Natala smiled; if he was sharing personal information then he couldn't be that bad. She allowed herself to relax before replying. "My roommate's grandma grew up there," She paused and frowned, "Well, I think she immigrated when she was ten. But she tells stories about growing up there. That's why I picked Italy to visit."

"It's a beautiful country. So much diversity, so much amazing food, and the language." Tony shrugged. "I disappoint my madre with how little of it I know but it is beautiful to hear the locals speak."

"I've only heard it spoken well on YouTube videos." Natala felt herself smile again. "But I had no idea what they were saying so I guess I wasn't the most impressed. My roommate uses some words, but she doesn't know too much and either way, she'd have no reason to speak it around me."

Tony opened his bag and pulled out a small book, then handed it to Natala. "Did you bring one of these?" He asked her.

Natala slowly took the book, studying it. "The English-Italian Dictionary." She shook her head slowly. "No, I didn't bring this one. I don't know how I didn't think about that. Kate wrote out some of the most common words she said that I would need, but it is definitely not this many." She flipped through the book slowly.

Tony grinned as he pulled out a tablet. "It's all yours for the flight. Gives you about ten hours, factor in the length of the flight plus takeoff and landing. That is, if you choose not to sleep at all, and you read while you are eating."

"Thank you." Natala smiled, opening the book to the first page. She pulled out her notebook and flipped to the back of the book, finding the empty pages. She pulled a pencil out of her backpack and began to file through the dictionary, jotting down the ones she thought would come in handy on her trip.

It reminded her of years ago, when she did the same thing with French words. Except this time, she was actually going to Italy. It wasn't just a plan for the future. It was happening.

Before she knew it, a stewardess was walking down the aisle of the plane handing out dinner trays. Natala carefully marked her place in the dictionary with a bookmark, then set that on top of her backpack at her feet. "I wonder what the meal is."

"A sandwich." Tony replied, stowing his tablet away. "I fly this airline a lot, it's normally a sandwich with some sort of fruit, crackers, and a pudding cup."

Before Natala could ponder this information, the stewardess was at their row, passing trays down. Natala looked at hers, noting Tony had been right. It looked like a very tiny sub sandwich, the lettuce on it starting to wilt. The fruit cut looked a bit more appetizing, there was pineapple, apple cubes, and grapes in it. A simple packet of two crackers and a vanilla pudding cup rounded out the food on the tray.

Natala opened the silverware provided, glad to find a wet wipe. She used that to wipe her hands, then picked up the sandwich. Good or not, it was her food and she paid for it, so she would eat it. She was surprised to find it wasn't bad, it tasted like a normal sandwich.

Probably because it is a normal sandwich, it's not like we are in space. An airplane can't be that much different than other places where you put a sandwich together. She thought to herself before taking another bite.

Natala must have been hungrier than she thought, because she'd finished the sandwich and fruit before she knew it. She looked at the crackers and the pudding cup, unsure if she wanted either. "Why are the crackers here? They don't seem to fit in."

"Insulting the crackers." Tony replied, popping a grape into his mouth. "They can hear you."

Natala couldn't help the laugh that followed. "But they don't go in the fruit, or on the sandwich, so they are just for eating on their own?"

Toney shrugged. "They probably have to include so many things or calories in the meals, so that's how they do it. Aren't you going to eat your pudding? Sugar is the best part."

Another laugh escaped Natala as she dropped the packet of crackers into her bag for later, in case she needed a snack. "Just because it's sugar? Vanilla isn't really a flavor I like; I'm pondering if it's worth eating."

Tony grinned and dropped his chocolate pudding cup onto her tray before taking her vanilla one. "I should have figured you were a chocolate girl."

Natala wanted to argue that, tell Tony he didn't know anything about her, but he was right. She was in love with chocolate, in any form. Besides, she wasn't about to lose this chocolate pudding that had been dropped into her lap, or really, on her tray. She opened the pudding cup. "Thank you." She said softly before she dug into the chocolatey goodness.

***

Natala felt a gentle shaking, and she rubbed her eyes before opening them slowly. When she saw a seat in front of her, she had to blink to remember where she was. "I'm on a plane." She said aloud.

"That you are." Tony - likely the one who had been shaking her - grinned. "You have been for hours now. You slept on a plane, which isn't something everyone is capable of. Great job."

Natala blinked again and reached for her water bottle. "I don't know if I'm really awake." She glanced at her watch, surprised to note there were still two hours before they reached Rome.

"Breakfast will probably be served in an hour." Tony informed her as he scrolled on his tablet.

Natala looked over at him, noting that none of his clothes looked wrinkled and his hair seemed to be in perfect condition. *He must not have slept,* she thought, *no one looks that good when they wake up.* She yawned, then picked up the dictionary Tony had lent her.

She opened the notebook, noting Kate's plans for today. According to this, Italy was seven hours ahead of Chicago. She would be landing at 15,15 local time. Natala frowned and blinked at that number. It didn't look anything like American time, which was likely why Kate had written her a note about it.

Italy uses 24 hour or military time. They also use a comma between the hour and the minute, where we would use a colon. Good luck :)

Natala frowned and bit her lip. She'd never used military time before, and math wasn't her strong suit. "So, twelve would be noon. Thirteen, fourteen, fifteen," She used her fingers as she counted, "would be three fifteen."

"What are you whispering about?" Tony asked in a whisper, almost making her jump. Her seatmate had grown on her during their flight, but she wasn't expecting him to reply to everything she said.

"Just trying to figure out the time. It's weird in Italy." Natala bit her lip again. "Or I guess they would say it's weird in America. Either way, it's a lot different."

Tony chucked. "I was raised using military time, it makes a lot more sense than all that AM PM stuff if you think about it."

"Maybe." Natala wasn't going to agree with that, so far it seemed like a lot of confusion. "We are going to land in Italy in the afternoon? But it's going to feel like eight."

"Jet lag is a well-known thing. Haven't you heard of it? You'll feel it at some point, probably when you try to go to sleep tonight only to find your body still thinks it's afternoon." Tony closed up his tablet and put it into his bag. "Do you know where you are going from the airport?"

Natala paused for a split-second, trying to figure out if telling him anything would be smart. He had been polite and helpful on the flight; he probably wasn't a bad person. "I have a cooking class to go to, it seems. Then a hotel to find. Or the other way around, I probably should drop off my things before I go cook..." She studied the notebook. "Pasta and Tiramisu." She read the name of the restaurant aloud.

Tony groaned. "Italian pasta is amazing. Any fresh pasta is delicious, but the Italians do it best. You'll love getting to taste the pasta even if you don't love the class itself. That's a great place to take a class, from what I've heard."

Natal grinned. "I am normally much better at the eating part than I am at the cooking part. I've been taught, but it's never really stuck."

"Hey, pasta can be sticky so maybe this class will stick. You can impress all your friends back home with what you learned." Tony told her with a grin of his own. "Looks like breakfast is headed this way. I predict oatmeal, another bowl of fruit, and a pastry of some sort."

Natala watched as they handed out trays, trying to tell what was on them so she could see if Tony was right again. She would have asked if he wanted to bet, but she was clueless when it came to airline meals.

Natala saw bowls, so maybe it was oatmeal. She brushed the wrinkles out of her sweatshirt unsuccessfully, then packed her notebook and pencil back into her backpack. She wanted to be ready to get off the plane when the flight was over. She set the dictionary on top of Tony's bag as the stewardess came to their row.

"Told you." Tony said as he handed her breakfast tray.

A bowl of oatmeal sat in the center, two tiny bowls next to it. One had raisins in it, one had some kind of brown fluffy stuff. There was a medium sized bowl of fruit that looked just like the ones they had been served for dinner the night before. A small biscuit and packet of jam were also on the tray. "Would you like any juice ma'am?" The stewardess asked her.

"I'll take orange juice, if you have it." Natala replied, then watched as the stewardess poured her some orange juice from a large pitcher and it was passed to her. "Thank you."

Natala took a careful sip of the juice, then tried not to frown. It tasted more like water than actual orange juice. She carefully dumped the raisins into her oatmeal, then glanced at the fluffy brown stuff for a moment before adding that as well. Whatever it was, it was obviously meant to go into the oatmeal. She had never been a fan of oatmeal, she remembered as she raised the spoon to her lips. Whatever would possibly make it taste a bit better, she would try.

Natala ate her breakfast slowly as she watched out the window, wondering if she was seeing Italy. She saved her fruit for last, to act as the dessert for her meal. It tasted just as good as it had last night. She finished just as an announcement came over the loudspeaker for passengers to buckle their seatbelts, as they would be landing soon.

Natala smiled as she buckled her seatbelt and handed her tray to the stewardesses who were quickly gathering them. They were almost to Italy; her adventure was really and truly starting. She remembered the elderly lady's words yesterday. She was starting her jump into the unknown.

Chapter 2

After she got off the plane and collected her luggage, Natala looked around the airport. She was shocked by how large it was. She even saw a lingerie store that was common in America, as well as many other stores and restaurants. She walked past many of them as she made her way out of the airport.

When she got outside, Natala noticed it didn't look that much different than America. She wasn't sure exactly what she thought it would look like. If the ground would be blue or she'd thought the sky would be purple, but it seemed so... normal. A sense of disappointment began to sweep over her. She took a deep breath. This was Italy, and she was really and truly beginning her adventure.

There were many people around, rushing in any direction. Natala looked at the map she had printed off her laptop before she left home, red dots marking the places she needed to be. "Okay, so I need to take a train." She said aloud, one hand tightly holding her suitcase, glad her backpack was strapped securely to her back. She looked around her, trying to note where the train station was.

Natala followed the signs that had a photo of a train engine on them, along with the group of people she'd watched exit the airport. When she got into the station, Natala pulled out her train ticket and carefully used one of the machines to validate it with the stamp.

"Oops, I'm sorry." Two younger girls giggled as they ran away from Natala. She frowned and patted her pocket, making sure her passport was still there. She'd put it into an inside pocket of her jacket, hoping that would keep it safe.

"It's the train! The train!" Natala smiled when she saw a little boy excitedly jumping up and down as the train came into view. Come to think of it, she hadn't been on a train before either. "Maybe I should make a list of firsts." She said aloud. "First time in Italy, first time on a train..." She was sure the list would grow as the vacation went on.

After Natala found a seat on the train, she opened her notebook to a blank page and noted her firsts. She decribed what her flight had been like, and before she knew it the train was stopping. Natala gathered her luggage and stepped off the train, then looked around.

She followed the signs out of the station, then pulled out her map again. She was hopeless when it came to trying to find things, maybe she should have had Kate describe them for her or send her photos. It took a couple minutes for Natala to find the hotel – which turned out to be only a block from the train station. She checked into her room and left her luggage there before venturing out of the hotel to walk to her cooking class.

This one took a lot longer to find, and Natala was glad she'd started her walk an hour early. She smiled when walked inside the restaurant.

"Caio! Welcome! How may I help you this afternoon?" A lady greeted her.

"I am here for a cooking class, pasta and tiramisu." Natala looked around the place, realizing it really was a restaurant. She'd been expecting more of a school, but this was a full-service restaurant. The delicious aromas of pizza and pasta were very forthcoming.

"Perfect! You are in the correct place, and right on time. Come ti chiami? What is your name?" The lady opened a binder.

"Natala Luna." Natala put her hair behind her ear to keep it out of her face as she continued to look around the restaurant. There were so many scents vying for her attention, each more tempting than the last.

"Right here! Let me show you where the class is held. We have a room just for classes." The lady led Natala behind the counter to a room. At first glance it seemed small, as there was already a group of people gathered there. The room also held three large tables and seats for everyone. "Your instructor, Arianna." The lady who had led Natala introduced, then left the room.

"Good afternoon! Where are you from?" Arianna asked her with a smile.

"America, the state of Illinois." Natala replied, looking around. The room had huge windows on two walls bringing in a beautifully natural light. She felt a wave of peace before the one of excitement could join.

"Wonderful! We are going to have a great time cooking together today, feel free to take a seat anywhere you would like."

Natala looked around at the stools, noting that everyone else seemed to be here in groups. She picked a stool beside a group of three women, and sat down.

The woman next to her smiled. "You'll love this class. I've come twice before. Even if you learn nothing, you eat wonderful pasta. That must be why I keep coming, I'm hopeless in the kitchen." She glanced at Natala's hair. "You'll want to put your hair up; Arianna doesn't like hair in the pasta."

Natala noted the woman's tight, neat bun. "Thank you." She replied gratefully as she pulled a hair tie out of her pocket. She gathered her hair and wound it into a bun, trying to make it look neat. It was probably a mess of a bun but at least it was contained.

"Alright!" Arianna smiled at the group. "We are going to get started, there may be a few more people joining us later. Feel free to grab a glass of prosecco, and I am going to give a quick history lesson before we begin making our pasta. First, I am Chef Arianna. I've been teaching classes here for ten years, and before that I was head chef in our restaurant. Which, if you get a chance to check it out, makes some of the best pizza in Rome."

Natala smiled; she could believe that based on the smells coming from the restaurant. She drank from her water bottle as she listened to chef Arianna, choosing that over the offered prosciutto. She'd never been one for alcohol, especially when she wasn't at home.

"Before we get into the art of pasta making, we need to begin with the sauces." Chef Arianna smiled at the group as she picked up a stack of cards. "Tonight, we are going to make two different sauces. She stood up and pointed to the other side of the room. "This side will be making a marinara and basil sauce, and this side," She gestured to the side of the room that Natala was sitting in, "will be making a four-cheese sauce. I have laminated cards for you to use while you are here, I do need them back at the end of class. The recipes will be sent to the email you used to sign up for this class with so you can recreate them later. Because we only have three and a half hours, we split into two groups to make the sauces."

Natala mentally noted that she would have to ask Kate to forward her the recipes. She was guessing that Kate had signed Natala up with her own email. "My four-cheese sauce group, let's begin. The four cheeses that are in your sauce today are..."

***

Three hours later, Natala left the class with a full belly and a newfound appreciation of pasta. "That was so much harder than I thought it would be!" A lady told the man she was with as the couple exited the store in front of Natala.

"I should eat as much pasta as I can while I am here." Natala said aloud. The class had given her a greater appreciation for all the work chefs did to make the pasta.

"Pasta I can get behind." Natala heard a snap of a camera as she turned to see who had spoken.

"Tony." She said, taking a step back in surprise. She'd told him where her class was being held, was he here on purpose? Or had he just happened to be walking by? Either way, she was glad to see him.

Natala frowned at that, where had that thought come from? She didn't know this man well. He was more familiar than the rest of the country, and something about him was almost charming.

"So, you're a professional pasta maker now?" Tony asked her as he looked at his camera.

"As if." Natala replied, looking at the city around her. She wasn't sure where to go now, the cooking class had been the only thing Kate planned for her. And local time it was around 8pm, which seemed late. It wasn't dark quite yet, but Natala was guessing it would be dark before too long if it was anything like America.

"I'm headed to a garden to get some photos of the sunset this evening. Interested in joining me?" Tony asked her.

Natala considered this as she looked around, realizing she didn't have any better ideas. Kate had told her to be spontaneous, and it seemed like Tony was able to be trusted. "A garden?"

"It's raised above the city so you have a beautiful view of the city. It is one of my favorite places to get sunset and sunrise photographs." Tony led her down a street. "It is a bit of a walk to get there, but we still have an hour before the beginning of sunset. And this weather is beautiful for a walk."

Natala pulled the elastic out of her hair so her hair was loose, then shook her head a bit so the curls would lay the way they were supposed to. "It is pretty out." She agreed, looking around. There were plenty of people out, but not enough that it felt busy or crowded as they walked. Natala marveled at how many hotels were around, it seemed like there was one on every corner.

"What do you think of Italy so far?" Tony asked her.

Natala blushed, remembering her earlier disappointment. "It doesn't seem too much different than home really. Many shops, and more hotels, but there are still lots of people. And green grass just like home, some different looking trees but they are still trees."

"To be fair, you are in Rome. Rome is a big city. Just wait until you get into the smaller cities and see the beauty that is Italian architecture." Tony told her as he walked. "And there are spots that are harder to find that are beautiful, sometimes you just have to go for a walk. The hidden gems, if you will."

Natala laughed. "I don't want to get lost on a walk. I have a terrible sense of direction," She paused and blinked, "Actually I just really have no sense of direction at all. And I don't know how many people speak

English, I don't know enough Italian to ask for help getting back to the hotel."

"You could always show them a picture of your hotel." Tony chuckled. "Or show them a map. If you have a map, the streets go the same direction and lead to the same place in every language." He turned right and Natala noted the street they were walking along was made of bricks or something. "This street is beautiful." She said in awe.

"Cobblestone streets." Tony told her. "They are all over Italy, or at least they used to be. More and more of them are being replaced by asphalt streets nowadays."

"Why?" Natala asked as she looked at the smooth rocks that formed the pathway ahead. The rocks were different shades of browns and greys, forming a beautiful gradient. "These streets are more unique than asphalt could ever be."

"There are problems with them when more impractical forms of shoes are worn. They become very slippery when wet, which as you can imagine causes lots of problems. Cobblestone streets now are more for pedestrian roads than anything." As Tony spoke, he turned around and snapped a couple photos of Natala as she admired the roads.

"So far, this might be my favorite part of Italy." She admitted. There was something almost magical about them, like they had some from a fairytale. It made her feel warm inside.

"Not the pasta?" Tony feigned offense at her statement. "You've tasted the pasta and think streets are better?"

Natala giggled. "To be fair, I helped make the pasta so I am sure it was nowhere near as good as the other pasta I'll eat in Italy. And unless it's chocolate; I'd choose a beautiful view over delicious food any day."

"I hope visiting an Italian chocolate maker is in that notebook of yours then. Italy does chocolate just as well as any other country, if not better." He winked. "I may be biased." Tony found a fenced area and pushed a couple of large branches out of the way. "This way, into the secret garden."

Natala bit her lip, wondering how she found herself here, at this moment. She was following someone she barely knew into a hidden area; in a foreign country no less. The moment was getting more fairytale like with a secret garden. She ducked under another leaf before it could hit her head.

"And here we are." Tony snapped a photo of Natala as she looked around the garden.

It wasn't what Natala thought of as a garden. There was no food growing and very few flowers. Instead, statues lay around the garden, along with what seemed to be many species of trees. "Is that a palm tree?" She asked as she looked toward the middle of the garden, walking around slowly. She didn't want to miss anything.

"It is a palm tree. They aren't native to Italy, but you have to admit they look like they belong here, don't they?"

"They are beautiful. I've never seen palm trees in person before, we took vacations as a kid but never to places where there were palm trees. And the Midwest isn't exactly a palm tree hotspot." Natala smiled as she looked at the one in front of her, noting that the leaves seemed even larger in person. Pine trees were the type she grew up surrounded by, and they didn't have leaves of any size.

"Over here, this is my spot." Tony climbed up a small hill. From the top you could see parts of the city. The sun was low in the sky, like it had been waiting for them to arrive before it set. "This is a great spot." Natala said. "I bet you show it to all the girls you meet on your trips."

Tony shrugged. "Of course, I have a spot in any city I travel to in case I find some girl I'd like to impress." He pulled out his camera and took a shot, then looked at it and played with some settings. Natala had never been one for photography, and she felt her attention waver.

She examined the garden around her, wondering at some of the statues. There was one of a person in a robe without a head, one of what seemed to be a table with only a cloth of some sort on it. It was hard to tell, as the entire thing was made of stone. What did they mean? She wondered.

As she looked toward where the sun was beginning to set, Natala smiled at the beautiful colors that the sky was beginning to turn. The colors of the sunset splashed colors of light onto the cobblestone streets, making for a beautiful picture. "I've never painted before, but I wish I had some paint with me at this moment."

"That's why I have a camera." Tony replied as he snapped a photo "Much less work than painting, and I get to have all my memories of these views and nature's beauty at my fingertips." He shrugged. "Helps that I make money off it."

Natala smiled in agreement. "Money is helpful for life. A needed evil, as some say."

"Il denaro apre tutte le porte. Or in English, Money opens all doors."

Natala bit her lip as she thought back to Christmas. "Many doors, not all of them." She replied softly, more to herself than to Tony. The pain of her breakup was gone, but there were still scars on her heart. She'd trusted and loved someone for a decade, her scars were deep.

Tony gave her a glance, but quickly turned back to his camera. "What do you do?" He asked her.

"To make money?" Natala asked with a smile. "I work at a factory. I'm mostly in quality control, so I watch the lines and make sure all the products coming off them are up to our company standards. Sounds boring and definitely can be, but it pays the bills."

"What would you do, if you could do anything in the world and have it pay your bills?"

As Natala thought of a reply, she didn't notice Tony had turned her camera to capture her. "I don't actually know." She finally said slowly. "I've never been asked that, I guess I never really thought about it. In my family honest work is honest work, it doesn't matter what you'd like to do."

When she turned and spotted the camera she blushed. "I thought you were here for a client, like on an assignment or something. Why are you taking photos of me?"

"The assignment was to capture the natural beauty of Italy. You seem to have plenty of beauty and you are in Italy." Toney replied with a grin, though he lowered the camera. He looked toward the sunset and watched the colors. "It's really something isn't it?"

"It is. I can't remember the last sunset I've seen that was this beautiful." Natala replied, not sure how to take his compliment. She didn't like the wave of happiness that had swept over her, didn't want her emotions to get involved in this vacation.

"When was the last time you watched a sunset?"

Natala frowned. "I don't know. I see them as I drive home from work some nights in the spring and fall, I love those drives. So probably a month ago or something like that."

"You didn't really watch the sunset though." Tony explained. "Here, this standing and looking at the colors, getting here before it really starts to set. Leaving as the sunset is over and walking home in the light of streetlamps, that's watching a sunset for real. A lot of us miss that in our day to day lives, just rush right past the sunset or don't notice it happens. That's part of why I love photography, I don't have to miss those moments. I get to capture them to make sure no one else misses the view, but they miss the experience."

Natala studied the man beside her, wondering where that deep thought had come from. Though how much did she really know him anyway? She had met him less than twenty-four hours earlier. She sighed softly, and watched the sunset. There was something peaceful about it, being the only people in the park watching as the sun went to sleep for the evening.

She looked at the ground beneath her, noting the green grass. Slowly, she lowered herself to sit down on it, thankful the grass was not wet. As she watched the sunset, she heard the soft snapping of Tony's camera in the background.

***

"Natala?" Tony asked awhile later.

Natala opened her eyes and blinked, wondering when she had fallen asleep. "I'm sorry." She apologized as she stood up with a sigh. "I didn't realize I was tired."

Tony shrugged. "Well, it is getting close to midnight local time. And your sleep on the plane probably wasn't the best rest you've gotten. Ready to head out?"

"Absolutely." Natala pulled her jacket closer to her body for warmth and realized she was hungry. She'd have to take from her stash back at the hotel. Kate had encouraged her to bring many, many protein bars just in case she needed them or wanted something to snack on.

Tony took her hand and led her out of the park. Natala realized it wasn't as dark as she would have thought. The streetlights glowed onto the cobblestone roads, lighting their way back. "Do you just run around the city all day and photograph random things?" Natala asked him, still holding his hand. There was something normal about holding his hand yet intimate at the same time, something she'd never felt before. Nolen had considered it poor taste to hold hands in public, so it was something she'd never done with him.

"Random things? I'm offended." Tony glanced at the camera he was holding in his other hand. "Nothing I capture is random, I can picture my photo in my head before I've even taken it. I have a list of places where I may end up, places that fulfill my client's requests, but I guess I never know exactly where I'll be. Adds to the fun of it all."

Natala shuddered. "I'm not good at that random stuff. Plans are a lot better, and having maps." She looked ahead of them. "I have no clue how to get back to the hotel, I'm terrible at directions and getting lost in a foreign country isn't my idea of a great time." She glanced at Tony, not wanting to offend him. "A beautiful foreign country, but to me still a foreign country."

Tony frowned for a moment. "How are you planning to get around for the rest of your trip? How are you planning to view the city or cities and not get lost?"

Natala smiled. "Hope and prayers. And maps, as stated earlier. I carefully follow maps so I always know how to get back."

"I have an idea." Tony was quiet for a moment as they walked. Natala noticed that they passed the restaurant where she had taken her pasta making class. It was still lit up, as if people were still there at this time of night. She shook her head in disbelief.

"Tomorrow morning, meet me in the lobby of your hotel at eight. I have an idea that will solve all your problems."

Natala raised her eyebrows as she noted her hotel was coming into view. Tony must really know his way around, to just be able to bring her back here so easily. "All my problems? That sounds like an ambitious offer."

Tony chuckled as he let go of her hand and opened the front door to the hotel for her. "Not all your problems, but at least your directionally challenged one. And your fear of getting lost. Meet me tomorrow."

Natala gave him a small smile, wondering why her hand felt empty now. "I'll do that. Goodnight." She said softly as she walked over to the staircase. Her phone buzzed as she walked, and she carefully unzipped her jacket and pulled it out. "Good evening." she greeted.

"Evening? It's 4pm. I just got out of work. Your flight went fine then?" Kate asked her.

Natala grinned as she walked up another staircase, then started down the hall to her room. "It did. I even slept and ate on the plane, and took that pasta class you signed me up for." She walked into her room and closed the door behind herself, then locked it.

"Did you? Are you going to cook pasta for me when you get home then?" Kate asked her.

"I'm sure by then I'll have forgotten everything I learned. And besides, no one can top your grandma's pasta."

"That's true, nonna makes a mean lasagna. And other pasta dishes, but her lasagna is just the chef's kiss." Kate giggled. "Now that you've sufficiently made me hungry, I'm going to get started on my dinner. I just wanted to make sure you got to Italy and the plane didn't like go down or anything."

"You sound like a worried mother." Natala pointed out. She took her water bottle and threw it onto her bed, then opened her suitcase and pulled out a protein bar.

"You wouldn't tell your mother, so someone had to make sure you didn't get kidnapped or mugged. Speaking of which, there's a message here from your mother asking when you and name we-don't-say are going to visit. You haven't told her about that?"

Natala frowned, not wanting to think about her family. This was supposed to be her time away from her real life. "It's not something I like talking about. I'll tell them eventually; it's not hurting anyone. I've got to go Kate, it's like midnight here and I need to get a snack before I get some sleep."

"Have fun! Oh, and send photos!" Kate called through the phone before she hung up. Natala couldn't help the smile that came across her face as she set her phone down on the nightstand. She wondered why Kate hadn't come with her on this trip if she was so invested. Photos were a simple request that Natala could handle.

She walked over to her luggage and pulled out a pair of pajamas along with her cosmetic case. She went through her nighttime routine quickly, then grabbed the protein bar again and took a bite.

As she ate, Natala pulled out her notebook and updated her list of firsts, adding *watch an Italian sunset*, and *take a pasta making class.* Then she looked at the page for tomorrow. She was meeting Tony at eight, then taking a train to Florence at ten. She looked around the beautiful hotel room. She didnt know what Tony had in mind but it seemed she'd need to have her things packed before eight. "I should probably get some sleep now while I can." She whispered as she finished her protein bar and went to go brush her teeth.

Chapter 3

Natala blinked and looked at her clock, surprised to see that it was only four. She blinked again, realizing that wasn't her clock, and this wasn't her bedroom.

It took a moment for her to remember that she was in Italy, on vacation. "Vacation," She whispered as she wiggled her toes. It had been so long since she'd been on a trip, she wasn't sure what that was even like. She was wide awake now though, so she may as well get up. Was that the jet lag hitting? What did jet lag even feel like?

Natala pulled her covers back and climbed out of her bed, then walked over to the window. She opened the curtains and looked out at the city, realizing it was still dark out. "What should I do now?" She asked aloud.

She closed the curtains, not wanting to see the darkness. After selecting an outfit for the day, Natala got showered and dressed. By the time she had finished her makeup and packed up her bags it was still only 5,30.

Natala opened the windows so the sunrise could stream through her window, then sat down in a chair. "Now I have, let's see, six thirty, seven thirty, eight." She counted on her fingers as she spoke. "Two and a half hours until it is time to meet Tony in the lobby. Should I venture out and try to find some breakfast?" Natala looked out her window and bit her lip. She wasn't sure when it was typical to get breakfast, and didn't particularly want to have to search for her way home. Hopefully the other hotels Kate had gotten for her included breakfast. Was that common in Italy?

"I could read that book I started while I was waiting for the plane," She said, then dug through her backpack for that book before laying down in the bed to read.

The next time Natala looked at the clock it said 7,56. "Oh gosh," She exclaimed, quickly closing the book and packing it back into her backpack. She set the backpack and her suitcase on the bed, figuring she would come back for them after she learned what Tony's plan was. After putting her phone and money into a zipped inner pocket of her black leather jacket, Natala picked up her reusable water bottle and put it into the holder she'd brought, then slung that over her shoulder. "Let's head out," She said as she grabbed the room key and walked down the stairs to the lobby.

When she got there, she was surprised to see that Tony wasn't alone. Beside him stood a woman, a little younger than Natala maybe. "Good morning." Natala greeted them both.

"Good morning, Natala. Natala, this is Elena. Elena, meet Natala." Tony introduced.

The woman smiled and gave Natala a hug. "It's so nice to meet you. You have a gorgeous jacket; I absolutely adore it." As Elena spoke, Natala understood for the first time what it meant when a person bubbled with excitement.

"Natala, I thought Elena could be your solution. The family she is nannying has family staying for two weeks and she is on a break, so she'd love to be your guide so to speak as you enjoy this country." Tony explained.

"I would just be pacing around the guest home otherwise; you are doing me a huge favor if you let me accompany you on this trip of yours. Besides, it has been years and years since I have explored without tiny ones trampling all over the place. It sounds much more peaceful just you and I." Elena moved her hands as she spoke, a fact that fascinated Natala. Both Elena and Tony looked at her expectantly.

Natala looked back at them both, not completely sure what she was supposed to do or say at that moment. "Sure?" She offered when neither said anything. "I'm not stupid, I won't turn down someone who knows how to get around or at the very least has a much better sense of direction than I do."

Elena jumped up and clapped her hands. "Oh, perfect. This is going to be so much fun; I can't wait." She linked arms with Natala. "So, Tony did not tell me much other than he had a friend who didn't want to get herself lost. I want to know everything, what are your plans while you are here, how did you get here, why Italy..."

"I do have a train I am supposed to take at 10,00." Natala said softly, slightly unsure how to handle this very bubbly woman. She'd been around plenty of talkative people but Elena just seemed to radiate energy. Most of the people she worked with in the factory were not that way. Natala didn't notice as Tony slipped out the hotel doors.

"Wonderful! Let's go catch a bar before the train, is your luggage upstairs?" Elena asked her.

"Yes..." Natala frowned. "A bar? I don't really drink. I mean there was that one time, but I don't often."

Elena laughed. "Not that kind of bar. In Italy, bars are what Americans would consider a coffee shop." She paused. "I should also warn you that the coffee here isn't the same as what you'd be used to in America. In Italy, a shot of espresso is considered a coffee." She led Natala out of the hotel lobby. "There are bars at practically every corner, we will go grab a coffee and a pastry before we grab our things and catch the train. Where are we taking this train to and what are we doing there? I can't wait to take trains without children bouncing around, it sounds like a dream."

Natala struggled to keep up with Elena's pace. "Florence." She huffed out. "My roommate planned one thing for me to do each day, and today that is to take a train to Florence."

Elene noted her out of breath state. "Oh, I'm so sorry, I walk very quickly. I don't really notice it, the children run more than they walk and I am very used to keeping up with them."

"You're a nanny? How long have you been doing that?" Natala asked her as Elena opened the door to a bar for them.

After Elena ordered in Italian and paid for their food, she handed Natala a very small cup and held a similar one herself. She drank it quickly, as if it was the juice in a communion cup. Natala copied this move, trying not to react to the sudden surge of caffeine and bitterness from the coffee. She usually loved the bitterness of coffee, but this was hitting the back of her throat.

Elena giggled as she handed Natala a pastry and led the way outside once again. "You'll get used to that. In case you didn't know, bars charge you extra to sit down and eat there. So, it is common to just grab your food and eat as you walk. That is a chocolate croissant."

"They say Americans can't stay in one place," Natala muttered under her breath before she took a bite of her croissant. It was delicious, the pastry was flaky, light and buttery. The chocolate just elevated the taste of the warm pastry. This was a breakfast she could get used to.

"It's great, isn't it?" Elena grinned. "I've been a nanny for, gosh, four years now?" She frowned for a moment, which Natala had to admit seemed like an odd look for the girl. "Right out of high school, I found out that this couple I knew needed a nanny and I'd been waiting for the perfect excuse to move. So here I am. It's been such a joy watching the little ones grow."

As Natala watched the girl describe her job, she realized that Elena was one of those lucky people who had found her dream job. She radiated happiness and excitement when she talked about it. She certainly seemed to have the energy to keep up with children.

Elena took a bite of her pastry, then groaned. "I always forget how good they are. Fresh pastries are so much better than frozen, remember that. If you ever wonder whether it is better to go out for breakfast or stay in, the answer should always be go out." She took another bite and ate it with her eyes closed, which concerned Natala a bit as they were still walking.

"So, this trip of yours. Your roommate planned it? Are you close to your roommate? Is she a relative or a friend?" Elena looked at her expectantly.

Natala took a bite of her croissant and let herself enjoy the flavors as she considered her answer. "She's not related to me; we both needed an apartment so we rented one together. It was cheaper with a roommate. Her grandma is from Italy so she planned some of this trip for me. She took care of the logistics and planned some activities, but told me I need to be spontaneous some of the time." Natala wrinkled her nose.

Elena grinned. "You aren't the spontaneous type? Children made me spontaneous. Any moment that can be spent looking at something random is one less moment I have to entertain them. And there is so much that can be learned from those moments."

"I like plans. And directions, they make things simple and I know what to expect." Natala defended herself before she took the last bite of her croissant.

"There is so much beauty in Italy to be spontaneous about. The flowers, the museums, the food, the people." Elena's eyes sparkled. "So Tony, you met him on the plane? He must have gotten to know you well enough to ask me if I was interested in guiding you around the country. I don't hear from him that often, so I was surprised he contacted me. Is there attraction there? Do you think he's cute?"

Natala's eyes widened at Elena's straightforward and pointed question. She was glad she'd finished her pastry, because she may have spit it out otherwise. "What? I have no idea, I didn't, I'm not-"

Elena giggled. "That means you don't think he's ugly." She noted. "I think he's into you. He was going to beg me to be your guide. I should have let him honestly, but I was too excited for the opportunity. I love exploring and this just sounded like so much fun. A lot more enjoyable than sitting around the guest house for two weeks."

Natala didn't realize her cheeks were red. "I'm not looking for anyone." She said firmly. "I'm not ready yet. I'm on vacation, it's a break from the real world."

Elena studied her for a moment. "This sounds like the perfect train story." She smiled. "First, we need to grab our things and catch the train. Here's the hotel!"

It didn't take long for their luggage to be collected or for the girls to find the train. After they both stamped their tickets, they boarded the train and sat down.

"Oh, I should get your number saved on my phone!" Elena exclaimed as she pulled out her phone. "That's so much easier than making sure I know your hotel and room number to call you there."

"I remember doing that as a kid, using the hotel phone was so much fun for really no reason." Natala replied as she entered her phone number and name into the contacts app of Elena's phone, then handed it back to her.

"Wasn't it fun? The children like to do that when we stay somewhere. They get a kick out of getting to call their parents and wish them a goodnight all on their own." Elena looked at Natala closely, making Natala wonder what she was trying to figure out. "I have a feeling there was a story behind you not being ready yet to date. Is that why you took this trip? Are you escaping someone?"

"Escaping." Natala snorted, almost wishing that had been the case. "Not even close there. He wouldn't care. It is the reason behind the trip, I guess. I always thought my first out of country trip would be my honeymoon." She glanced at Elena, noting she seemed to be listening very closely.

"I was dating a guy for an embarrassingly long time. I always thought the engagement was right around the corner, I mean we talked about it all the time and everything." She bit her lip. "So, on Christmas when he didn't propose, I called him out on it."

Elena looked at her. "And he ended it?" She asked.

Natala snorted again, then covered her nose. "No, no he didn't end it. He said I needed a better job, needed to better establish myself, all that crap. I told him I was done waiting and left." She shrugged, hoping it seemed like that had been an easier decision than it actually was. "Kate told me I should take a trip on my own, and planned it out for me."

"Your roommate, right?" Elena asked. At Natala's nod, she asked another question. "So have you spoken to the guy since?"

Natala sighed. "Not a word. That's the crazy part I guess, that I thought I was in such a great relationship. That an engagement was happening soon, and then he didn't even care when I left. Kate says I was better off, but it's hard to believe that when you've spent a decade planning a future with someone."

"That's rough." Elena looked out the train window. "Italy is the perfect place to date. If it doesn't work, you can just go home and leave them a country away. Like you said, it's not your real life. And their accents," she used her hand to fan herself, "I mean it doesn't get much better than that."

Natala laughed as she looked around them, noting the train wasn't very full. That was okay with her. Two and a half hours was plenty long to be on a train no matter how many people were around. "You don't have an accent, but you speak what seems to me like flawless Italian and seem at home here. Where are you from?" She asked Elena.

"I'm from here and there, a bit of everywhere." Elena laughed. "Not really. I was born in America. My parents were not together, I've never been sure of the entire story there. It isn't talked about in my house. Somehow my madre ended up with me." She shrugged, a smile still on her face. "My madre sent me to Italy for the summers to spend them with my padre, and I fell in love with the country. My padre passed when I was sixteen, and I always knew I wanted to end up back here. I feel closer to him, so when a nanny position came up it seemed perfect." Her eyes sparkled. "And it has been wonderful. Probably not perfect, but wonderful and I get to stay in this beautiful country that has become my home."

Natala watched the younger girl, a bit of envy creeping up on her. Elena seemed to have known the direction she had wanted her life to go and she had accomplished that for herself. Natala wasn't even sure what her life was anymore; she just worked at a factory and had a great roommate. She didn't know what to do next, if there was even a point in staying in Illinois. She wasn't happy with her life, but she wasn't upset about it either.

She pushed a piece of hair behind her ear and reached into her backpack for her book. She glanced over at Elena to notice she had put in headphones and was listening to something on her phone. Natala smiled as she opened the book and began to read.

***

Natala got lost in her book and it seemed like a few moments later the train arrived in Florence. "We are here!" Elene exclaimed as she pulled her ear buds off and looked over at Natala. "Did your roommate make you hotel reservations? Do we have a certain place to go or are we off to find a random hotel?"

"Yeah, I have an address for the one she booked me a room at." Natala felt the excitement wash over her as she put her book back into her backpack. She pulled out her notebook, then zipped the backpack back up and grabbed her bag before she followed Elena off the train. "Here." She said, handing Elena the notebook.

"Oh, that's a beautiful place in Florence. You'll have a great view." Elena handed Natala her book back. "Let's go there first, we don't want to travel around the city with luggage. It makes us a target, and that's not something we want. I'll see if they have an available room for me, or I'll stay at a different hotel nearby."

Elena started to lead the way from the train station. "What else do you want to do today?" She asked Natala.

"What do I want to do? I have no idea." Natala replied, surprised that Elena was asking her. "I thought that you were the guide." That would help with the spontaneity, if Elena was the one making the decisions.

Elena giggled and shrugged. "Yes, but this is your trip. I want you to enjoy everything we do, not just to follow you all over the city."

"I just want to see the country." Natala said as she looked around them with a smile. "And eat all the food, I've heard some great things about the pizza, and I'd love to try some pasta I didn't make. Oh, and gelato. I have heard amazing things about Italian gelato."

"Gelato." Elena looked up at the sky and sighed. "I love gelato. We should definitely have a lot of that, like way too much. I'll be able to eat it without worrying about how I will get the children to fall asleep for their naps." She grinned. "I should warn you; this will be a long walk. I think we should make it to the hotel, unpack, then reward ourselves with gelato. The most adorable little gelatory is only a couple blocks away from the hotel."

Natala was starting to wonder what wasn't adorable in Elena's mind. "That sounds perfect." She agreed, excited to find out what the hype was behind gelato. She looked around, noticing there seemed to be plenty of cars, as well as buses around them. "Why are we walking instead of taking a taxi, or a bus?" She asked her guide.

Elena paused for a moment, almost causing Natala to walk into her. "I don't know." She replied as she began walking again. "I'm just so used to walking, I guess I didn't even think about a bus or a cab. They cost, and walking is great exercise, so I'm quite used to walking." She explained. "Plus, if I take the children somewhere in a cab, they fall asleep. If we walk, then they lose energy instead of gaining it. I really need more reasons for things than my job."

Natala smiled and shrugged. "I don't mind walking. But if my legs start to shake, I may need you to carry me."

Elena laughed loudly, causing another group of people to look over at them. "I'm definitely not strong enough for that. You'll make it. We can walk slower if you'd like. And remember, gelato is the reward. It is so worth it."

"Gosh, that would only make this walk last longer. We can keep going at this speed. How much of Italy have you been to?" Natala asked Elena curiously. She quickly realized that there were many different things to see and do in Italy, yet Elena seemed to have done all of them. And knowing exactly how close the gelatory was to the hotel seemed a bit more than common knowledge.

"Goodness, I think I've been to a lot of it. The family that I nanny for travels often and I accompany them, taking care of the children so they can go out for dinner and such on the vacation. And when I was little, my father took me to see many different things." She smiled. "How much of America have you been to?"

Natala bit her lip as she tried to calculate. "I'm not sure. I've been to maybe thirty of the states, but of course I haven't seen all of each state." She blushed a bit. "I see what you mean."

"It's easier with Italy in a way, Italy is something like a thirtieth the size of America. But there are still those great hidden spots I am sure I will never be able to find in certain cities, where I know them well in my own city." Elena shrugged. "There's this park, back where I lived with my padre for the summers. It had the prettiest flowers and I used to go there every afternoon to smell them. Maybe you know a similar spot in your hometown."

Natala nodded. "This coffee shop, back in Wisconsin where I grew up. They were this tiny family-owned place, but they made sure to have many drinks for us children. My mom had all the fancy coffees and I got to have a fancy hot chocolate right along with her. Different flavors and decorations and such." A warm feeling came over her as she reminisced on her childhood.

"See? Everyone has their spot." Elena turned a corner. "It would be really cool if everyone in a certain city or area came together to write a book including all their spots. Imagine all the stories, all the cool places you'd be able to learn about."

"Sounds like the perfect pro ect to start the next time you are bored and you don't have an American to guide around Italy." Natala offered.

Elena's eyes sparkled in the sun. "I'll have to keep that in mind." She replied. "Here is your hotel, let's get you checked in and see if we can find a room for me." She opened the door and led Natala inside.

Natala's eyes widered as she noticed a huge chandelier in the entrance. It was bigger than she was somehow. And the chairs were all white leather, they looked super fancy. Natala frowned, how much had Kate spent on this place? It seemed like a very expensive hotel. She looked at the notebook that she held to confirm this was the right place.

The name matched, so it must be. Kate had booked her three nights at this place, so she'd have to hope that came with a deal or something. *This is vacation, stop worrying and just enjoy it.*

"Natala! Come, they need your information. There are some open rooms, they can try to put ours close if they have your reservation information." Elena called.

Natala walked over to the check in counter with a smile. Trust Elena to have already charmed the lady behind the desk.

After they'd checked into adjoining rooms, which according to Elena were hard to find, the girls headed down the street to find some food. Elena was determined to have some gelato, but Natala had said she was too hungry to start with that.

"Here we are, you'll be able to check something off your list. Pizza." Elena flashed her a smile as she opened a door and led Natala into the restaurant. "Do you like to order your own food or do you mind if I do it? I'm so used to ordering for everyone with the kiddos, it's easy enough if you don't mind."

Natala shrugged. "Go ahead. I'm sure you know much better than I do what is best at places. I'll eat pretty much anything, unless it's spicy. I can't handle spice."

Elena nodded. "No spice. Noted." She looked around the restaurant. "Why don't you go grab a table and I will bring the food. It's getting busy here. It's so wonderful to see, I love when my favorite places are busy. That means they won't be closing anytime soon."

"Okay." Natala agreed, amused by Elena's take on things. The girl seemed to be an optimist. Natala walked a bit into the mess of tables that were present in the restaurant before she could find an empty table. As she sat down, she noticed there were people eating many different foods around her. This must not only be a pizza place then.

She couldn't wait to try all the different foods Italy had to offer. Other than spice, Natala had always been one to try everything she could find once. She'd once tried octopus. It wasn't her favorite, but she could say she'd tried it. When she was a child, the menu had always been the same. Eating out was a huge rarity because of her brother's allergies.

"Pizza!" Elena sang as she sat down across from Natala and set a plate in front of her. "So, this isn't your ordinary pepperoni pizza. This is a pesto pizza. There is pesto, mozzarella, oregano, and tomato. It sounds a bit weird for pizza, but it is going to surprise you with how good it tastes."

Natala's mouth started to water. "That actually sounds delicious, I like pesto."

Elena took a bite of her slice and nodded in agreement. Natala picked up her slice and took a careful bite, surprised by how hot it was. She carefully finished that bite then took a long sip of water. "I have to let that cool, it must be really fresh."

Elena nodded. "It is, that's what makes it so amazing."

Natala laughed and blew onto her pizza before taking another bite. She could taste most of the components of the pizza, the tomatoes, pesto, and mozzarella. She wasn't sure exactly what oregano tasted like but it was most likely there. "You're right, it is amazing. It's going to ruin frozen pizza for me if I eat too much of it."

"You could always learn how to make it." Elena suggested in between bites.

Natala looked at the slice she was holding as she ate it. "I'm not a good cook, and by that, I mean I really can't cook. Maybe with a frozen or like premade crust I could do that, but I think it would ruin the purpose."

"You'll figure it out. Maybe you haven't found the right class or the right cookbook yet. Or the right type of food to make. Cookbooks really are amazing." Elena looked at her pizza. "Keep eating, the gelato awaits us." She encouraged.

Natala laughed, then took another bite of her pizza. Once both girls finished, they headed down the block to the gelatory.

"I'm going to warn you, there are so many flavors it's hard to pick." Elena told Natala as she opened the door to the gelatory. "Lots of flavors sounds like I'm going to end up eating a lot of gelato while I am here." Natala replied as she walked into the gelatory before Elena.

She looked around, noting the long counter that held tubs and tubs of gelato. It looked very similar to the ice cream shops he had been to back home. There were tubs inside a counter, and each was covered with a metal cover. "What is the difference between gelato and ice cream?" Natala asked Elena, then blinked. Elena was no longer behind her.

"Elena?" Natala asked, looking around the shop with a frown. A wave of fear washed over her; she didn't see Elena anywhere. Where had she gone? What was Natala supposed to do now?

"What can I help you with?" The man behind the counter asked her. Natala bit her lip, that was one question answered. The next thing to do was order gelato. She glanced at the flavors quickly. "I'll take the double chocolate please. The smallest size you have."

"Of course." The man grabbed a cup from a stack behind the counter and put a scoop of the chocolate gelato inside, making Natala's mouth water despite her nervousness of being alone. After she paid, he handed her the cup and a spoon. "Thank you." Natala smiled, then left the shop. She glanced down the streets, trying to figure out where Elena had gone.

"Can't waste good gelato." She said aloud as she took a bite of the sweet treat. She sighed and closed her eyes as the sweet, rich taste of chocolate hit her mouth. "Elena was right, it is amazing." The gelato felt light in her mouth, and not as cold as ice cream.

"Right about what?" Elena asked as she suddenly appeared beside Natala, her cheeks looking flushed.

Natala looked at her, unsure what to say. "Right about how delicious gelato is. You didn't get any though. Where did you disappear to?"

"Oh, um, I just saw something I needed to check on. Come on, let's go to this art museum I know about. You can't come to Italy and not see any art." Elena took off at a very fast pace, leaving Natala almost running behind her as she tried to enjoy her gelato.

"That was really weird. At least I'm getting a workout today," she said to herself, glancing at the cup of gelato. "And chocolate. Chocolate makes everything better."

Chapter 4

As Natala sat in her room the next morning curling her hair, she was still wondering about Elena's momentary disappearance. The girl had been less energetic the rest of the day, and it seemed like she was always looking behind herself.

Natala carefully untwisted her hair from the curling wand, then smiled when she saw the curl had turned out perfectly. Today, she and Elena were going to some kind of market that Elena said she would love. It sounded like a farmer's market to her, but Elena had been quite excited. She said she would meet Natala in the lobby at 9.

As Natala wound her hair around the hot iron again, she glanced at the clock. It was already 8, and she hadn't heard any movement coming from Elena's hotel room. Maybe she was one of those people who didn't need much time to get ready in the morning.

Natala's phone vibrated, making her almost jump. "There is a hot piece of metal way too close to my head for you to scare me right now phone." She reprimanded the device. After she'd unwound her hair from the iron and set it down, she picked up her phone.

Good morning, beautiful. This is Tony. I'm doing another sunset photoshoot tonight, this time in a garden in Florence. Are you interested in joining me?

Natala frowned and looked at the text. How had Tony gotten her number? Was it posted online somewhere? Her mother had always warned her about keeping personal information off the internet. Or maybe Elena had given it to him? That was the only answer she could come up with. Unless he had searched for it online or something crazy stalkerish.

Sure, I'd love to watch the sunset again. Natala typed back, excitement building. She once again picked up her curling iron to finish getting ready for the day. "I wonder what firsts I'll be able to add to my notebook today. Yesterday I tried gelato." That memory was a great one for Natala, she couldn't wait to try more.

As she walked down to the lobby a half hour later, she noted there were more people at this hotel than it seemed there had been in Rome. *This really must be a high-class place or something,* she thought. *It makes me feel special, like I'm an important person.*

"There you are!" Elena exclaimed. "So, the best part of this beautiful hotel, or one of them at least, is that they serve breakfast! We can go grab some food there before we head out. It's so easy and quick and hopefully delicious." She glanced at Natala. "Great water bottle holder, where did you get that? It would come in handy while I'm chasing the kids."

Natala laughed as she followed Elena. It was as if yesterday's disappearance and aftermath had never happened, Elena seemed to have all her energy back. "I got it on Etsy." She replied. "It has definitely come in handy."

As the girls entered the breakfast room, Natala blinked. The breakfast looked exactly like the ones she remembered having on family trips as a child. A different country, yes, but it seemed there were some things that were the same. She picked up a plate and grabbed a pastry that looked like it had chocolate in it, along with a banana.

Elena grabbed a plate and started to stack pastries on it. Natala watched her incredulously; the girl had to have at least six different ones on her small plate.

"What?" Elena shrugged. "I have to try everything. There are six different flavors, how will I know which is my favorite if I don't try them all?" She led Natala to a table and set down her plate, then flitted away.

Natala couldn't help the smile that came to her mouth. There was something about Elena that just made her laugh, the childish innocence she seemed to have and her eagerness for life. Natala picked up a napkin and spread it over her lap to catch any crumbs, then picked up a pastry.

"They have apple juice." Elena gave a satisfied sigh as she set two cups down in front of her on the table. "I could live here." She picked up the small cup of what Natala was guessing was coffee and drank it quickly.

Natala eyed Elena's plate once again. "It's a good thing we aren't going to be here for too many days, you'd eat the hotel out of business." She replied.

Elena shrugged as she studied her pastries, then broke one in half. "I like to get my money's worth." She said before taking a bite of her breakfast. "Strawberry." She identified, looking at the red filling in the middle.

Natala ate her own food slowly, savoring her pastry. Elena wasn't a fast eater, so she had plenty of time. The curls she had done today made her hair shorter, and it kept touching her chin which seemed so strange to her.

"This one is my favorite so far. Blueberry I think, that's the one you should go for tomorrow." Elena commented, holding half a pastry out for Natala to see before she finished it.

"Sounds delicious." Natala replied, silently thinking the chocolate one sounded a lot better than blueberry. Why would someone choose fruit when they could have chocolate? Even better, add the fruit to the chocolate.

"So, this market thing today, how far of a walk is that going to be?" Natala asked before wiping her fingers on a napkin.

Elena twitched her nose as she finished her pastry. "Five miles or so." She replied. "That's around eight kilometers, the metric system's equivalent to miles that is used here."

Natala's eyes widened. "Five miles? Do I look like I am in shape enough for that?" She set her napkin down on the table, suddenly wondering if she should have had a bigger breakfast.

Elena giggled as she brushed her hands off. "You'll do fine. We can go slow and there are plenty of delicious places to stop at for a break along the way. Gelato, pasta, pizza, and that's only the beginning." She replied as she picked up her plate, then took Natala's. "I'll just add these to the dirty stack, then we can be on our way."

Natala glanced at her water bottle, suddenly wishing she had a couple more of them. She wasn't a walker, didn't go on hikes like ever, so five miles seemed like quite a bit to her. Maybe Elena should have just told her eight kilometers, she wouldn't have known how far that was.

"Ready to go?" Elena asked her with a smile.

"Ready as I'll ever be." Natala replied as she stood up slowly. "Let's go find this market thing. Why is this a thing I will love?"

"Oh, because they sell everything." Elena walked quickly out of the dining area, leaving Natala to almost run behind her. "Like your jacket, there are plenty of leather workers there. Jackets, wallets, purses, bookmarks, all handmade and they are so unique. I could spend an hour just looking at everything."

Natala bit her lip, doubt filling her. She had never been one for shopping. Goodwill was her favorite store; she could just search in her size for the color she wanted and find something that would work to wear and hopefully be on style. Her leather jacket had been a gift from her siblings this year, with hidden inner pockets because they were worried about her getting pickpocketed if she got too close to Chicago. Hopefully Elena wouldn't need to look at everything, because it certainly sounded like that could take a while.

"There are also food vendors." Elena smiled at her. "They have some really good and unique treats there. Like chocolate, I think you especially would love all the chocolate. Oh, and they are very knowledgeable too. If you want to know how long something will last, feel free to ask. And if you'd like to take something back home, they are pretty knowledgeable about what can and cannot go across the border. Or if something needs to be packed a certain way to go across the border, like be vacuum sealed, they can usually tell you that too. I love getting unique foods and sending them to my madre."

"I didn't even think about taking something home with me. I should probably be thinking about souvenirs." Natala mused. "I definitely should get something for Kate."

"Your roommate?" Elena asked.

Natala nodded. "She'd love to try some of the food, so that could be perfect. I'll have to keep that in mind while I am looking at everything."

"It's a big market." Elena told her. "I think you'll find more than you even knew existed. You'll need a second suitcase to take back everything you could find."

Natala laughed. "That's the best part. I want to find all the best things from Italy so I can take a bit of the country home with me. Except for the chocolate, that isn't going to make it home."

***

When the girls arrived, Natala was surprised to see that Elena had not been exaggerating about how big the market was. It seemed to be the same size as the local mall growing up, with two stories. "The outdoor part of the market is the handmade goods, and indoors is all the food." Elena told her when she noticed Natala was looking up. "So, we should probably go there last. It's where the money leaves quickly."

Natala laughed. "I'll follow you. Where should we start?"

"Let's do a circle, stick to the rule of right. That way if one of us gets ahead of the other we should be able to catch up easily enough." Elena decided as she walked over to a tent and picked up a leather purse. "See? This is what I was telling you about. Look at how perfect this stitching is." She said softly to Natala.

Natala ran her finger along the stitching of the purse. "It's beautiful." She replied, looking around the booth. There seemed to be many different colors of leather, something Natala had never taken the time to really think about.

She picked up a small leather wallet that said Made in Italy across the front in a simple font. She opened it and looked inside, noting how well it seemed to be made. Maybe it would be good for her brother, he was still using a fabric wallet he'd gotten as a child as far as Natala knew. Natala looked at her jacket and smiled. Besides, her siblings had gotten her something made from leather, it was a cool coincidence.

"How much?" She asked the lady who seemed to be manning the booth. "Eighteen euro." The lady told her. Natala considered the wallet, mentally trying to calculate how much that was in dollars, and if it was worth it.

"A little over twenty dollars." Elena told her softly. Natala hadn't even noticed her, but was thankful for the help. "I'll take it." She decided.

She paid for the wallet and carefully put it into her water bottle holder, knowing it would take a half hour to pry out later but no one would be able to take it. "Now that I got something for my brother, I have to find something on this trip for my sister." Natala told Elena.

"There are so many different places to look. If you don't want something made of leather, Florence is known for its goldsmiths and all the gold jewelry." Elena suggested. 'And then again, there's always the food."

"That sounds like a great place to look. I don't have to find anything today either; my trip still has a couple days left." Natala laughed as they moved on to the next booth, another leather maker.

It took them the entire morning to look through all the booths at the outdoor market, and Natala had found a necklace for her sister at one of the goldsmith booths. "Now for the best part." Elena grinned at her. "We have to find something to eat."

"How are you hungry after all the pastries you had for breakfast?" Natala asked as she looked around at all the food vendors. There were so many different ones, how was she supposed to pick only one thing to eat? Chocolate was obvious, but that was dessert.

"Oh, I can eat a lot of food when I want to. Especially when it is as delicious as this." Elena replied. "Let's get some lunch before we do food shopping, then we will be less hungry and less likely to impulse buy."

"That's a great suggestion." Natala agreed. "But how are we supposed to make a decision on what to have?"

"Oh, that one is easy." Elena grinner. "Just follow your nose, and try whatever smells the best."

Natala blinked. While it sounded like an absurd way to find lunch, it also somehow made sense.

Elena looked at her expectantly. "Where does your nose lead you?" She asked.

Natala closed her eyes and let the smells of the market wash over her. She could smell pizza, pasta, fish, cheese, and that was just the smells she could identify. She opened her eyes and led Elena over to a booth in the back corner that seemed to be selling pizza. Even though she had already tried pizza in Italy, it just seemed to be calling her over.

Elena smiled. "Neapolitan pizza, you have a good nose." She wrinkled her forehead. "Forget I said that, it sounded weird as soon as I said it aloud. But that's a great choice, it's delicious pizza and you will love it."

"Neapolitan pizza? Is that like a dessert pizza with strawberries, vanilla, and chocolate?" Natala asked.

Elena giggled. "Not even close. It gets its name from its origin - Naples, Italy. It is said to be the original pizza, and Naples the place where Pizza was invented. In some places it is just called Neapolitan-style and made similarly, but this is the real thing. The dough must be made a certain way with certain flour, and a certain type of mozzarella cheese is used. I think the tomatoes are specific as well as the cooking time." She smiled. "It also doesn't seem like it has any toppings, but trust me, it's delicious. Ready to try it?"

"I'm always ready to try pizza." Natala agreed, letting Elena lead the way and order the pizza. Natala paid for both slices, then took the paper plate she was handed. Even that plate seemed better quality than a normal paper plate. As Elena led her to a table, Natala inspected the slice of pizza she'd been handed.

Elena had been right that it didn't seem to have many toppings, it was simply the sauce, some cheese, and basil. It smelled divine. She slid into the seat across from Elena, then took a bite of her pizza.

The lack of toppings wasn't noticeable as she ate it. Her mouth was filled with the yeasty taste of freshly baked crust, mozzarella cheese, and fresh tomatoes. The basil enhanced all the tastes she already had and just seemed to be the cherry on top of the pizza.

"It's the best, isn't it?" Elena took a bite of hers. "They have margarita pizza in America as well, but it is nowhere near this good. You need the fresh taste, and the Neapolitan style is as authentic as it gets."

"I could eat this every day." Natala replied with a small giggle. "It's really good."

"There are so many pasta dishes that you'll love after you try them. You will have plenty of things you want on a daily basis." Elena used a napkin to wipe some tomato from her face. "And right now, you can find treats to take home with you."

"That reminds me that I have to go home." Natala groaned. "This is like a whole other world, where I don't have to work."

"Like a vacation?" Elena asked with a raised eyebrow.

Natala sighed. "Like a vacation. I suppose it makes sense that I am on vacation."

"You're on vacation?" Elena's eyes widened playfully. "I had no idea. Maybe you need a guide and friend to go on this vacation with you." Both women laughed and stood up. They threw away their garbage, then began to browse the food stalls.

Natala and Elena shopped at the market, then watched a movie at the hotel before they went out for dinner. Natala got her first taste of Italian pasta not made by herself and had to agree with Elena. There were many things here she wanted to eat every day. The chocolate was just as delicious as she'd expected, and she had bought enough to last the rest of her trip.

Now, Elena had gone off to do who knows what and Natala was getting ready to meet Tony in the lobby. "Do I need to fix my hair?" She asked the mirror, looking at the curls. "They are a little frizzy, but we are going to be outside. It's probably fine." She sprayed a little bit of water on her hair and smoothed it down. "That works." She popped one of her chocolates into her mouth, savoring the flavor. This one was infused with rose water, giving it a light rose taste that just seemed to bring out the chocolate even more.

Natala added a bracelet she'd bought herself from the market earlier, than looked at the clock. "And I'm running behind." She noted, grabbing her water bottle and making sure it was full, then running out the door.

Natala considered using the elevator for a brief moment, then realized it would probably not be any faster than walking because she'd have to wait for it. She headed down the stairs and entered the lobby, still not used to the huge chandelier.

"Good evening." Tony greeted her.

Natala smiled. "Good evening." She echoed, silently laughing at the formality in that greeting. "How many sunset photoshoots do you do?"

Tony led her out the door, holding it open for her. "Many. There is something special about the sunset, those photos always seem to be the most popular. I try to get as many as I can, and it's a great excuse to watch the sunset many times over."

"You have watched the sun set in many different countries then?" Natala asked as she walked out the door, then let Tony take the lead. *It would be nice if he'd hold me hand again,* she thought, wondering where that had come from.

Tony shrugged. "I guess I have. Never really thought about it, but the sunset is beautiful from any country. It's one of those things that doesn't really change, no matter where you go. Unless you go to Alaska in winter, then there are no sunsets to watch." He turned a corner.

Natala smiled as she followed, noting the cobblestone streets she was walking on. "Now it sounds like you're speaking in fairy tale language or something." She said with a laugh.

"Fairy tale language? That's the first time I've been accused of anything like that." Tony glanced at her. "You haven't said much about yourself. What do you miss the most about America."

"What do I miss the most?" Natala repeated the question slowly and bit her lip as she thought about it. "I'm really not sure. It feels like I am so far from it. And I haven't been here too long to miss anything." She shrugged. "That wasn't really a real answer."

Tony watched her as they walked. "It was a real answer, you aren't super tied to anything back there. Nor are you adverse to trying new things from the sounds of it. Why haven't you traveled sooner? Or have you?"

Natala sighed, wondering that herself. "I haven't before this trip. Routine, I guess. I had a routine and a life I thought was great, so I had no reason to travel. And I was saving my money for a wedding." She shook her head. "So much for that."

"You were engaged?" Tony asked, raising his eyebrows.

Natala gave a self-deprecating laugh. "No, I wasn't. I thought that's where we were going after ten years of dating but he thought differently apparently. So, I'm no longer with him, and my roommate told me I should take a trip."

"Ten years?" Tony whistled. "If ever it takes a guy that long, he doesn't really want to marry you. The dating is convenient so he will stick with that. He's biding his time until someone else comes along that he does want to marry."

Natala shrugged. "That probably explains why I haven't heard from him since." She glanced at Tony. "What made you start travel photography? Going all over the world for work instead of staying in one place and creating a routine?"

Tony chuckled. "Routines are boring." He told her, leading her into a grassy fenced area. "There's a lookout here, I want to climb up to that to get some sunset photos. You aren't afraid of heights, are you?"

"Nope. Not really afraid of anything. Well, except snakes. I don't do snakes." Natala told him.

"Great. It's over here." Tony led her to a ladder and began climbing it. Natala carefully followed him, making sure she didn't slip. Ladders could be slippery; she was glad this one wasn't.

When they got to the top, Natala saw it was a platform with railings around. She looked down, not sure how high off the ground they were.

She sat down on the platform, feeling too tired to stand as she could still see plenty while she sat. "You dodged the question earlier." She pointed out. "About why you do travel photography."

Tony looked out from the platform and was silent. Natala was beginning to wonder if she'd get an answer, or if he was just ignoring the question.

"I married my high school sweetheart." He said finally.

Natala's eyes widened. *He was married?*

"We were young, only eighteen. We started at the same college and had a pretty normal life. We weren't rich in money but we were rich in happiness." He paused, and Natala watched as he looked out at the city. "Then one evening, she realized there was a lump in her right breast."

Natala heard herself gasp. Tony glanced back at her with a sad grin of understanding. "That was about my reaction. Stage four breast cancer, it was too late to do anything. She had six months, and we decided to spend it traveling. I could go to college later." He shrugged. "I took photos while we were in England. Photos of her that I took for myself. Photos of the scenery as well, because it all seemed so magical to two nineteen-year-olds."

Tony picked up his camera as he continued to speak. "After..." He tried off, then snapped a couple of photos. "Later, someone saw my photos and offered to sell them at his gallery. They sold quickly and he asked for more. I never looked back, it seemed like something she would have loved for me to do and I had no ties in America without her."

Natala watched as he continued to photograph the city, unsure what to say. It seemed like such a sad story, and he'd always seemed like a cheery person. It gave her a small window into his mind, into how his life wasn't as picture perfect as it may have seemed – pun intended. *His vulnerability was attractive,* she had to admit.

Tony glanced back at her again, and she met his gaze. "It's been a while now Natala. Life continues. I have a dream job and I never had to finish college." He grinned. "Always thought I lucked out in that department; school was never my thing. Once they see my photographs, no one seems to care that I'm technically a college dropout."

"You did more college than I did." Natala offered, as she twisted her bracelet around her wrist nervously. She didn't notice that Tony snapped a photo of her, then of her bracelet. "I never even started."

"Did you want to?" Tony asked her.

"I think so. It seemed like the normal thing to do, like I was weird for not going. But I couldn't afford it and I didn't want to have the debt from it to have to pay off for years and years. I guess I never really knew what I would have gone for either." Natala replied, still fidgeting with her bracelet.

"You could always go now. I mean if it's still something you wanted to do, a regret of yours, it's never too late to get a higher education." Tony suggested, camera still in hand.

Natala gave him a smile. "I know. But I still don't have anything I'd like to go to college for, so it doesn't seem worth it. Besides, I think they say the longer you've been out of school the harder it is to go back."

"I believe that." He watched her. "You work in a factory, is that what you want to do with the rest of your life?"

Natala laughed. "I don't think so. But working at Regan Foods is stable and I can make a living," She looked around, "I can even make enough to take a vacation to another country. It's really not a bad place to work. And the city is nice too. Far enough from Chicago I avoid some of that craziness. I always thought I'd be a mom; I'd have kids sooner than later."

"You could have kids, you know. Marriage or a partner isn't really required anymore."

"I couldn't do that. I was raised to get married before I have children, I don't want to disappoint my parents." She was quiet for a moment, realization hitting her. "Maybe that's why I haven't told them about the break-up yet. They keep asking when I'll be engaged."

"How long ago did you dump the guy?" Tony asked her, still taking photos.

Natala looked at the sunset, the colors just as beautiful tonight as they'd been in Rome. "Five months ago, my birthday. Christmas."

Tony whistled. "That's a heck of a double present."

Natala tried to hold back her smile but she couldn't. "That s what my roommate said. She got me chocolate cake and brought her grandma's Italian lasagna."

"Your roommate sounds like a great person." Tony said as he walked away from the railing and sat down beside Natala. He lay back and looked at the sky.

"She is." Natala agreed as she lay back and looked into the sky as well. "It really is beautiful." She whispered to herself.

Chapter 5

A faint ringing was coming from the hall, Natala ran towards it. Someone was chasing her, but she couldn't tell who or why. "NO!" She screamed as she felt a hand touch her arm, then all she saw was darkness.

The ringing was getting louder now, and Natala opened her eyes. Her heart felt like it was beating out of her chest. She looked around the unfamiliar room, the ringing still in her ears. She blinked, realizing the beeping was coming from her phone.

Natala reached for it and turned off her alarm, then groaned and lay back on her pillow. "I'm in Italy." She reminded herself. "This is the hotel. That was just a really weird dream." She frowned as she looked up at the ceiling. She didn't often have dreams, much less nightmares as that had seemed to be. "Weird." She whispered.

Natala felt her phone vibrate, and she looked at the screen. It was the reminder she'd set for herself to accompany the alarm, telling her to get out of bed and get dressed. Natala groaned as she sat up in her bed. Today's Kate-planned activity was a hot air balloon ride over southern Tuscany. However, in order to get to that balloon ride when it took off, she had to catch a bus at three am.

"Why Kate, just why?" She asked aloud as she got out of bed and gathered some clean clothes to put on. There was no time to shower or do much for makeup, so simple it was for today. Of course, she could have gotten up earlier to do either of those things, but sleep had seemed a lot more worth her time. The hot air balloon would only fit a dozen or so people according to the lady Elena had spoken to yesterday, so not that many people would see her anyway.

Natala made quick work of changing and mascara, then threw a brush through her hair before carefully and quickly pulling it into a side braid. "There." She said as she looked at the mirror. "Perfect." She grabbed her water bottle and threw it over her shoulder as she left her hotel room. As much as she didn't want to be awake in this moment, she also couldn't wait to experience a hot air balloon ride.

"Good morning!" Elena grinned as she closed the door to her hotel room. "Ready for our early morning adventure? I've never been in a hot air balloon before, I'm so excited. I can't wait to be in the air and see what everything looks like from above. Of course, I've seen the world from an airplane but that's so high up in the air you really can't see much. A hot air balloon will be a perfect view."

Natala groaned. "Of course, you are perky and energetic in the morning. Can't you tell some people haven't had their coffee yet?" She asked as she walked over to the elevator and pushed a button.

Elena looked her up and down. "Unless I've missed something, you don't drink much coffee. You normally choose juice over coffee at breakfast time, when traditionally a coffee would be the choice. You've had one coffee the entire time I've been around you, while I've had like three a day. I'm thinking your problem isn't coffee."

"My problem is that it is three in the morning. Why do busses even run at this time?" Natala asked as she stepped into the elevator. She wasn't about to squelch the girl's excitement, but truthfully Elena's energy was making her even more tired than she'd been before. She'd rather be quietly excited.

Elena followed her in. "I have no idea really. They don't stop, I guess it's good for overnight riders? Or people who work odd shifts?" She shrugged. "It works out well for us today. Otherwise, we may have had to take a bus last night and sleep outside as we waited."

"Yeah." Natala replied she watched the doors to the elevator close. She was lucky there had been an extra spot on the hot air balloon she was taking, because otherwise she'd have spent the day without her guide. And a bus ride at this time by herself wouldn't have been her favorite thing to do in any country, much less an unfamiliar one. Was having a guide still following Kate's plan for spontaneous adventures?

"Have you ever been in a hot air balloon before?" Elena asked her as they got off the elevator.

"Nope." Natala led the way out of the hotel. "I've seen plenty before, but I've never been in one. When I was a kid, we went to these hot air balloon shows where a ton of them were lifted off the ground and others landed there. Some had cool designs or were shaped really cool." She walked down the street. "This way, right?"

When there was no answer, Natala turned behind her and noticed Elena had disappeared. "Not again." She groaned, looked out into the dark streets. "It's not even daytime. I have zero energy for this." She was too tired to be concerned, too tired to do much other than figure out how to get on the bus by herself. She'd done it once before on the day she'd gotten here, so surely, she could do it again.

Natala walked back into the hotel and noticed a couple men by the check in counter, but didn't see any other people. Elena had just vanished, disappeared the same as she had outside of the gelato shop. Was she a ninja or something?

Natala closed her eyes then looked up, taking a deep breath. "I'm going to try to make it to the bus stop. It's five blocks away, I know how to get there." She whispered, hoping no one else was listening to her. She left the building again and started to walk down the sideway.

After she made her second turn, she was surprised to see Elena standing there, as if she'd been waiting for her. "Where did you go?" She asked, feeling a bit of anger.

Elena ignored her question. "Let's go." She said, and took off at a pace Natala had a hard time following. Natala frowned, *what was happening? Why was Elena disappearing; and why was she walking so fast?*

She stamped her bus ticket after Elena and tried to keep up with her as she boarded a train car. Natala sat down beside Elena and watched the girl. Her eyes were on the bus's door and she seemed almost jumpy, like her energy had turned into something else.

"Do you think the hot air balloon will be colorful?" Natala asked, Elena's eyes not leaving the train doors.

"I don't know." Elena replied absently, never moving.

Natala looked over to the doors in case there was something interesting happening there, but she saw nothing. Just people boarding the bus, and only a few people at that. This was the most deserted bus she'd seen. "What are you watching?" She asked.

Elena blinked and shook her head as the bus doors closed. She turned to Natala. "Hm? Oh, nothing." She smiled. "Now there is only a bus ride away from us and this hot air balloon." She frowned. "And a cab the rest of the way."

Natala bit her lip. Elena hadn't said that with the energy or excitement she'd had at the hotel. Something was off, but Natala was completely lost on what that could be. She looked out the bus window and watched the city go by as Elena closed her eyes and leaned against the back of the seat to take a nap.

A bus ride and cab ride later, the sun was just beginning to rise as they walked over to the hot air balloon. As soon as they got into their cab, Elena had gone right back to the energetic, excited girl she usually was. Right now, the hot air balloon just looked like the biggest picnic blanket Natala had ever seen on the ground, with a basket beside it.

"Good morning!" A lady walked over to them, holding a clipboard. "Are you registered to go for a ride this morning?"

"Yes, I'm Elena and this is Natala. I talked to someone on the phone yesterday and made my reservation then, and Natala's had one for a while." Elena told the woman, almost bouncing up and down as she spoke.

Natala laughed at Elena's eagerness. She felt the same inside, but wasn't quite awake enough to bounce as the younger woman was doing.

"Wonderful!" The lady made a mark on her clipboard. "Follow me over here, and you can watch the balloon being inflated. Matt is starting that process right now." She gave them another smile before walking over to another couple who had just arrived.

Natala and Elena looked at each other and grinned before they walked over to the balloon. Natala felt like this was a once in a lifetime opportunity. How many people got to fly in a hot air balloon? She was glad Kate had picked this activity for her.

"Natala, it's gigantic." Elena whispered loudly.

"It really is." Natala watched as the balloon was spread out on the ground, getting larger and larger by the moment. "There were twelve spots, right? And there has to be a pilot, or whatever the person who drives the hot air balloon would be called. It has to be a big enough balloon to keep at least thirteen people in the air."

"I don't know how I haven't done this before!" Elena squealed. She paused. "Actually, I do. It's because I wouldn't want to bring children along for a ride in the sky, that would be stressful." She grinned. "This, this is not stressful. This is the best thing ever."

"Elena, I think I found your weakness. You would do anything for a hot air balloon ride." Natala told her as she watched the girl hop up and down in excitement.

"Not anything. I just had to pay for a ticket and now we are here and we are going to go into that balloon." Elena took a couple deep breaths, closing her eyes as she did so. "I am calm." She declared, folding her hands together.

Natala raised her eyebrow, not believing that for a second. She glanced around them and noted more people had arrived to watch the balloon inflate and go inside it. She set the windbreaker she had brought with her on the ground, then sat on it to watch the balloon get ready for their ride.

"I feel like I can see the entire world from here." Natala told Elena softly a half hour later. They, along with the other people in their group, were now in the air. The pilot had explained that he had no clue where they were going this morning, the wind told them that. All he could do was raise and lower the balloon as needed. The wind was what moved them across the city and determined their route.

It sounded a little scary to Natala, but she figured that the pilot knew what he was doing. This company had to be good too, or Kate wouldn't have set it up for her to do. Natala decided to focus on the flight and not think about what could go wrong.

"It's beautiful." Elena whispered back. "Look at how tiny the buildings look from up here. It must still be too early for people to be around, because I can't see any of them."

"The buildings still look so pretty, it's like a mini village you'd see in a painting or something." Natala frowned. "A little village from above. Maybe that's not a normal painting concept."

"I don't care if it is, it should be. Look at all the fields, from up here they look like gardens." Elena pointed to one that was beneath them. "That one especially, it's like a square garden shape."

Natala laughed. "Square garden shape? I think gardens can be any shape."

Elena shrugged. "Square ones are cooler. We are going to land in one of those."

"We still have a while before landing, don't wish this to be over any sooner than it needs to be." Natala said. "Think of how small we look from below. I remember always thinking hot air balloons could only hold like one person inside the basket, but this basket is huge."

Elena glanced back into the basket. "I don't know if huge is the right word, but there is certainly enough room for all of us. This is the best thing I've ever done." She said as she pulled out her phone to take pictures of the world beneath them. "Smile Natala!"

Natala grinned as she grasped one of the handles inside the wicker basket and Elena took her picture. The pilot had said the handles were there for them to hold onto during the landing, but Natala felt safer holding on to it all the time. She was also nervous about her phone falling out of her hand and down to the city or a field below, so it was staying zipped away in her jacket.

"I'll text you all my photos when we get back to the hotel or somewhere with service later." Elena told her as she put her phone back away. "You have to have some at least to remember this experience by."

Natala looked below with a smile. "I don't know how I could ever forget this experience. It is probably the coolest thing I have ever done." She made a mental note to send some of the photos to Kate. She was happy not to have her phone out, it gave her a chance to be present in the moment and enjoy the experience.

Her mind went to Tony for a moment, she wondered if he'd ever captured photographs from a hot air balloon. They would be some really cool photographs if he had. But camera equipment was expensive so maybe he hadn't wanted to chance that so far above the ground. Maybe if he hadn't, she could convince him to go with her sometime.

Natala blinked as that thought made its way into her mind. What made her think they would spend more time together? Especially after she was back in the States?

They floated across the city for an hour before Matt, their pilot, landed the hot air balloon in a field. Natala was surprised to find that landing felt as smooth as it looked, they just floated down to the ground and that was it. She carefully got out of the basket and went to stand beside Elena. "Aren't you glad we could get another ticket so you could come with?" She asked as the other people in their group got out of the basket.

"So glad. This is possibly the coolest thing I have ever done. Seeing the tiny buildings, seeing the tiny fields, it was all so beautiful." Elena agreed. "Now for the hard part, we have to help get that huge thing into that tiny looking bag." She glanced over that the bag Matt had taken out of the basket, that supposedly would fit the fabric part of the balloon once they folded it.

"After we finish, they bring us brunch." Natala reminded her. "Think of how much you enjoy brunch."

"I hope coffee is involved. I'm starting to feel that early leaving time." Elena glanced at Natala. "I'm surprised you are still standing. How late were you out?"

Natala blushed. "I got back at 23,00." She replied. "I had like three hours of sleep, it's something. You're the one who fell asleep on our bus ride."

"Like I said, coffee. It's needed. You should really try it more; it would give you so much more energy and we could move faster." Elena replied as they were called over to grab part of the balloon and help fold it up. It made Natala break a sweat, and she realized it may not have been a bad thing to skip her shower this morning because she would definitely need one when they go back to the hotel. Together and very much with the pilot's direction, they did get the balloon back onto the bag that seemed so small compared to the balloon.

And sure enough, when they were finished the van had arrived and set up a brunch for the group to enjoy before they went back to the takeoff spot. "Food sounds so good right now." Natala said as she put a pastry on her plate and took a cup of orange juice from the table.

"I hear you, there is nothing like a pretty morning and hard work to make you appreciate food." A lady who was across the table replied with a grin. "It was a good reason to wake up early."

"I second that!" Elena held up her cup of coffee in a toast, seemingly reenergized from the coffee. "I'm going to make this a yearly tradition or something now. I'm 100% doing it again on a regular basis. As much as I can get away from work and afford it."

"I wonder if there are any hot air balloon trips in America." Natala mused before taking a sip of her juice.

"There has to be somewhere." A man replied from a different spot at the table. "I live in the middle of nowhere in Arizona, so I'm guessing nowhere close to me. But somewhere in America there has to be. California maybe."

"I live not too far from Chicago. Maybe there would be something in my area, it's a bigger city." Natala said. "Something I will have to look into when I get back."

"Have you been enjoying Italy so far? We saw the leaning tower yesterday, and it was pretty cool. I've seen it so many times in photos that seeing it in person seemed unreal." The lady across the table asked Natala.

"It's been a wonderful adventure so far." Natala said, silently making a note to check the notebook and see if Kate had planned for her to visit the leaning tower. It was such a known thing in Italy, she was guessing it was part of the plan.

"What kinds of gelato has anyone had?" Elena piped in. "Everyone has had to eat a scoop of gelato, right?"

Natala laughed and took a bite of her pastry as the conversation turned to food.

***

As they traveled back to their hotel in Florence, Natala noticed that Elena seemed to lose her energy the closer they got to the city. She began their cab ride full of excitement about the hot air balloon ride, looking at all her photographs and talking about how excited she was to do it again.

She'd gotten quieter when they got on the bus, talking about the little buildings but not sounding very enthusiastic about it, her eyes constantly darting around the bus.

Natala filed this in the back of her brain, not sure what it meant. "What do you want to do for the rest of the day? We only have one more day in Florence."

"I'm kind of tired, I may just take a nap at the hotel." Elena told her as she watched out the windows of the bus, not meeting Natala's gaze.

"Okay." Natala replied slowly. "Do you want to go out for dinner and gelato later? I'd like to find that chocolate covered cherry flavor they were talking about this morning."

"I'm not sure, it could be fun to order room service. We haven't tried the hotel's food other than breakfast, which was pretty good." Elena suggested.

Natala looked at her, not sure where to go or what to say next. Elena turning down gelato seemed like such a weird thing. In the day she'd known Elena, she'd discovered food was one of her weaknesses.

"Room service would be a cool thing to try." She agreed after a couple moments. "I don't think I've ever gotten room service, so it would be a check off the list of things I've never done. And I can maybe finish that novel I brought; I haven't had too much time to read while I've been here."

"Sounds like a great plan." As their bus reached their stop, Elena gave her a small smile. "Race you to the hotel."

Natala's eyes widened as Elena rushed off the bus and off the bus stop. Clearly Elena hadn't been kidding about racing. It seemed a little too fast to walk to Natala, she was basically running. "It's like she wants someone to think she robbed a bank or something." Natala said, thinking back to the many episodes of crime shows she'd seen that began with someone running out of a station of some kind.

She followed Elena at a much slower pace. A pace so much slower that she couldn't see Elena at all. She walked by a gelato shop, then stopped on the sidewalk. "If Elena is just going to take a nap..." Natala smiled to herself and opened the door to the gelatory. "When in Italy." She whispered. "Eat gelato."

"You had the same idea we did!" Two elderly ladies that had been part of their hot air balloon group followed Natala into the gelatory.

"All that talk about the different flavors made me hungry." Natala smiled at the pair, wishing that she could remember their names. "What flavor are you going to get?" She asked as she surveyed the flavors, disappointed to find chocolate covered cherry wasn't among them.

"Pistachio for me, I had it last year and haven't been able to stop thinking about how delicious it was." One lady laughed and put her hand on the other lady's arm. "Candace always has chocolate, she's never been one for adventure."

"I enjoy adventure very much, just not when it involves my food." Candace told Natala, giving the other lady a glare. "Gloria just has a more adventurous sense of taste than I do. She always has, ever since we were little girls."

Natala studied them for a moment, trying to figure out if it was rude to ask. "Are you sisters?" She asked, deciding if they weren't, maybe the fact that she had thought they could be was a compliment.

Gloria laughed. "Was it that obvious?" She asked as Candace walked up to the counter to order. "We are, twins in fact. We don't look like it though, do we?"

Natala looked between the two. "I wouldn't have guessed the twins." She agreed. "I should have though; my siblings are twins."

"Come join us and talk for a while once you order your gelato dear." Gloria encouraged Natala as Candice brought two scoops of gelato over. "It's always exciting to meet new people."

"Okay." Natala agreed. She ordered a cup of pistachio gelato, deciding to try it out. She carried it over to the table Candice and Gloria had claimed. "You said that you came here last year, do you travel often?"

The sisters looked at each other and laughed. "We travel almost all year now." Candice told her with a smile. "We are both widows now, neither of us had any children."

"You just travel the world together?" Natal asked. She tried to think of her sister, wondering if she could travel the world with her. She immediately thought no, her sister would never be up to that. "Of all the places you've been, which has been your favorite?" She asked as she sat back in her chair and took a bite of the gelato, ready to hear all the stories these sisters had to tell.

Chapter 6

The next morning, Natala was the one who was extra excited. She and Elena were taking the train to Pisa, then they would be touring the city on Vespas. Technically they were called mopeds, but she thought Vespa sounded so much more Italian. It was also a whole lot more fun to say.

Natala tried not to get too excited as she browsed the breakfast buffet. She grabbed a strawberry flavored yogurt to go with her normal pastry and orange juice. "I wonder if the next hotel will have breakfast." She said aloud.

"You'll have to visit the bars if it doesn't." A familiar voice said. Natala turned around and grinned at Tony. "Good morning." She greeted him as she passed him, searching for a table to eat at. "I haven't heard from you for a moment." She should have been surprised to see the man, but somehow, he seemed to find her wherever she went.

Tony followed her and sat down across from her. "I was working late hours. You seem to be in very good spirits today."

Natala couldn't hold back another smile. "Kate's suggested activity for today is a Vespa tour. I guess that's the stereotypical thing I've seen when I think of Italy, and I can't wait to try it out."

"Have you ever been on a moped before?" Tony asked as he fiddled with his camera. "Or motorcycle?"

"Nope. Only cars, boats, trains, airplanes, buses..." Natala trailed off and took a bite of her pastry. "Oh, and horse. I've ridden horses before."

"You have a lot of transportation methods left to try. Camels and elephants, horses are just the beginning." Tony told her.

"I went in a hot air balloon yesterday, so this trip I'll have tried out two new transportation methods. I've added many things to my list of firsts. I'd say that's pretty good." Natala eyed him curiously. "What have you been doing on this trip? I mean I've seen you here and there and I am assuming you are taking photos, but where?" She laughed at her rhyme. Somehow her eagerness was translating into extra energy.

Maybe that was how Elena had been so energetic so early yesterday morning.

"Gardens mostly. And there is a particular art gallery here in Florence that I've been contracted to take some photographs for. That is where all of my hours yesterday went. I believe they will be using them to update their website and for marketing." Tony explained. "I have one more day before I'm finished with that, so I'll be watching the sunset here for one more evening."

Natala took a sip of her orange juice. "I'll be spending two sunsets in Pisa, then one on a plane before the rest are spent in America." She said, realizing that her trip was more than half over. It seemed like it had just started, there was still so much to explore. And so much gelato to eat. She'd loved the pistachio yesterday and couldn't wait to see what Pisa had to offer for gelato flavors.

"I'll have to try to catch the sunset with you in Pisa tomorrow night then. One more Italian sunset before you leave." Tony looked around the hotel. "I should probably head off to get my photographs before anyone finds out that I'm not actually a guest here."

Natala laughed. "See you tomorrow." She called as he walked away. She looked back at her plate, realizing she hadn't eaten any of the yogurt yet. "Did I really want this?" She asked herself. Maybe she'd just seen the strawberry on the label and wanted to try something healthy. Her stomach was so full of nervous excitement she wasn't sure she could wat anything else.

"Want what?" A girl asked her as she slumped into the chair Tony had just left. Natala stared at her, then blinked. "Elena?" She asked.

"What?" Elena asked, seemingly having no idea why Natala was confused. She looked over to the breakfast buffet tables. "I need to get some breakfast before we catch the train."

Natala blinked again as Elena stood up and walked away, wondering what was happening to her. Elena's hair had been brown yesterday, and today it was blond. Had she dyed her hair in her hotel room yesterday? Had that been her reason for being so mysterious on the bus? Why was Elena not acknowledging it?

"All my stuff is waiting behind the counter in the lobby. Whenever you grab yours, we will be ready to catch the train to Pisa." Elena gave her a huge smile that didn't seem as real as her usual smiles as she set down two coffees and a pastry. "You texted that Kate had planned for you to do a Vespa tour today?"

Natala tried to ignore the strangeness she felt and regain her earlier excitement about the Vespas. "Yeah, I think it's a four-hour tour around Pisa. It sounds like a lot of fun."

"Vespas are a great way to get around Italy." Elena agreed. "That was one of the first things I did when I moved here, after I got my international driver's license. I'd ridden enough mopeds in the US that I was fully prepared. It was a blast. So much smaller than a car and easier to find a place to park." She drank one of her coffees.

"I will never understand Italian coffee." Natala commented as she watched Elena down her second one. "There's no enjoying the flavor or trying out new coffees or lattes. Just get a shot of espresso, drink it, and bam, that's coffee."

Elena giggled, the first glimpse of the real Elena that Natala had seen this morning. "It makes some sense when you think about it." She replied, picking up her pastry. "It's a quicker way to get the caffeine boost, and you don't have to carry a cup around with you that never quite gets finished."

"But the flavors and even the roast types, like I watched my mom spend hours in the coffee aisle growing up. She had so many different flavors and different days she'd want a darker roast than others." Natala drank the last of her orange juice.

"I have some peppermint mocha coffee at my place." Elena whispered to her. "I get it from America sometimes, because I do get what you mean." She frowned. "Although spending a couple hours in the coffee aisle sounds very excessive."

Natala shrugged. "I agree. I can get in and out of the shop a lot quicker than that, but my mom is particular. I'll go grab my things so we can catch the train." She told Elena as the girl took another bite of her pastry.

"Sounds like a plan." Elena agreed, not meeting Natala's eyes. Something still seemed wrong to Natala, but she had no idea what to do about it. She decided to try to ignore it and enjoy her Vespa tour instead.

***

"Look at that! It's just like in the pictures." Natala breathed as Elena slowed their Vespa. There were three other people on the tour, each on their own Vespa. Natala had been the only one in this particular group who couldn't drive, so she'd had the option to be Elena's passenger or the tour guide's passenger. She was very glad Elena was driving, the girl seemed to have a very good knowledge of the scooter.

"It's unreal, isn't it?" Elena asked as their tour guide started to talk about the history of the leaning tower of Pisa. Natala wasn't really listening, she just wanted to look at the thing. There was something about being here, about seeing it with her very own eyes, that was amazing. Just like the lady had said yesterday. "Why haven't I been traveling my entire life?" She breathed, thinking of all the other places that would be more beautiful in person.

Elena laughed. "That's a question I cannot answer for you. Make it a goal for the rest of your life then. This could be the first trip of many."

Natala silently vowed to do just that. This trip had taught her not to wait around for things to happen, she'd spent too much of her life doing that. "I was in my relationship for way too long." She said aloud, admitting what she'd been thinking for a while now.

Elena turned to look at her. "That seems like a random thought."

Natala sighed as she looked back over at the tower. "It's been on my mind, now that I'm here and feel so disconnected from normal life. I kept waiting. Just waiting to make enough to buy a house, waiting to be engaged and have a family. Waiting for my honeymoon to travel, I was just in a state of waiting. This, now, is living. I want to keep doing this."

Elena was quiet, they both pretended to listen to the tour guide talk. "Relationships are complicated." She said softly enough Natala wasn't sure she had heard her right. "Let's head to the right." Their tour guide said, and off they went again.

Natala loved the feel of the wind in her hair as she looked around at the buildings in this city as they passed them. Secretly, she thought she was the luckiest one on this tour because she got to look around and enjoy the ride while everyone else had to focus on driving.

They stopped next at a cemetery. "This, along with the baptistry we saw beside the tower, is the most visited place by high school students. The story goes that as many times as a student walks around the baptistry is the grade they will get on their exam." The tour guide said.

Natala frowned as she looked back at the baptistry. Going around that a hundred times? That seemed like it would take days. "It would also take someone who doesn't get bored easily." Elena added, as if she'd been reading Natala's thoughts.

"I could never." Natala said as the tour guide explained it was what students called a great excuse to skip school. "Did you ever skip school growing up?" She asked Elena.

Elena shivered. "I could never." She laughed as she repeated Natala's words. "My madre would have killed me, that's why I could never come to Italy during the school year. It wasn't worth it for a couple days and I was not going to miss school just for a visit."

"I can relate." Natala frowned. "Well, not to the Italy part. But I don't think I ever would have considered skipping school; my parents would have been furious. 'You're the oldest child, you have to set a good example for your little siblings.'" She looked at Elena's back. "Do you have any siblings?"

Elena didn't answer her, Natala wasn't sure if she'd heard. "Off we go again." Elena as she followed the tour guide away from the cemetery.

When their tour was over, the girls went back to Corso Italia, which apparently was a very known street in Pisa. It was filled with shops, restaurants, and bars. "There has to be a gelato shop somewhere around." Elena commented as they walked. "That's where I want to end up. I think I'll treat myself to two scoops today."

Natala laughed. "I can't wait to see what different flavors they have. I may have to enjoy two scoops as well, just so I can try more of the flavors. I think gelato has ruined ice cream for me."

Elena gave a happy sigh and looked into the sky. "There's just something about gelato that gives it an extra," She shrugged and waved her hands as she searched for a word. "Special something." She laughed. "Did you know that Gelato is just Italian for ice cream? It is the ice cream of Italy, but shouldn't be confused for American ice cream."

"Really?" Natala frowned. "I didn't know that; it seems so different from ice cream. That special something you mentioned, I think it's the lightness of gelato. It seems like I could eat a million scoops and not get full."

"Really. There are differences in the recipes, I don't know all the specifics. Mostly the same ingredients but different proportions. Gelato is considered richer than ice cream." Elena giggled. "It's also served like ten degrees warmer, so maybe it's the lack of brain freeze that contributes to that special something."

Natala watched her, wondering how long the happy energetic Elena was going to be around. It seemed now that she had two completely different personalities, like at times she was an energetic innocent young lady. Other times it was like she was jumpy and ready to hide at any moment.

The sudden change of her hair color still struck Natala as odd. Elena was also wearing her hair differently than normal. Before today she'd always left it down, but today it had been coiled into a tight bun since they left the hotel.

"I'd like to check out the shops too, if it's anything like the market we went to the other day. I got gifts for my siblings and treats for myself to take home, but I haven't found anything for my parents yet." Natala said as she looked at all the shops that were around them. "And I've already eaten the chocolate stash I thought would last me the rest of my trip, so I need to stock up on that."

Both girls laughed. "Are you going to get something other than food for your roommate?" Elena asked.

Natala bit her lip. "I'd like to, but I'm not sure yet what it should be. It's like I need the perfect thing, she planned this entire trip for me. But I haven't found that perfect thing yet."

"Maybe you'll find it today!" Elena bounced up and down. "There, let's check out this one. Leather, that always makes me think of you."

Natala looked down at her jacket. "I can't imagine why." she said dryly.

"I just want to look at everything again. I don't normally get to shop, if I do any going into stores it's very quickly. The children don't have a long attention span, and I'm also always worried they will break something." Elena picked up a leather bracelet and ran her finger along the surface. "I like to at least glance around whenever I get a chance."

Natala looked around. "I don't think too many of the things in this store would be that breakable."

Elena shrugged. "Perhaps not, but at other places they are and I was generalizing."

Natala smiled as she looked at the purses the shop had. The prices seemed so high, probably because she didn't normally buy things made of real leather. Her purse back home was fabric of some kind, not even fake leather. "This is such a crazy thing for people to be able to make." She said to Elena as she looked at the stitching along the end of the purse. "There are so many seams and every stitch is so even, I could never do anything like that."

"It takes a lot of patience and learning." Elena agreed as he came over to look at the purse Natala had found. "Think of how cool it would be to be able to make something like that, I'd love to just walk around with a purse I made."

"I think I did that when I was in third grade." Natala put the purse back and followed Elena out of the shop. "It was a class project, we made purses out of paper plates. I think we used yarn to sew them together, I can't remember exactly. But I carried that purse around everywhere until it started to fall apart. My mom said I'd tell the cashiers that I made my own purse when she took me grocery shopping."

"I wonder if I ever did anything like that." Elena said softly.

"Your mother never tells you stories about you as a child?" Natala asked.

"Not really, we don't talk much anymore." Elena gave her a fake smile. "Time differences and all."

"That's too bad." Natala replied. "I don't talk to my mom very often either. But whenever we get together, she loves to share stories about what my siblings and I were like as children. She could tell you when I lost my first tooth."

Natala looked down the street, then blinked. "Is that a Sephora?" She asked incredulously. "I thought I saw one in the airport, but I figured I'd imagined it."

Elena looked down the street. "Looks like it!" She laughed at Natala's face. "An international brand, they are all over the globe, I think. At least in Italy and America, I haven't really done much traveling outside of that."

"We have to check it out. If nothing else, I want to be able to brag about going to a Sephora in Italy." Natala laughed as she glanced at Elena. "I'm probably acting like a typical tourist, aren't I?"

Elena shrugged as they walked over to the Sephora. "Doesn't bother me. As long as we find a gelatory before too long, that pasta we had for lunch seems like so long ago."

***

Later, in her hotel room for the night, Natala was enjoying a cup of hot chocolate and getting ready for bed when her phone buzzed. The hot chocolate in Italy was very different from the hot chocolate that America had, it was so thick it reminded her more of soup than a drink. The thing they both shared was the deliciousness of the chocolate.

Where are you watching the sunset from tonight? Tony had texted.

Natala smiled as she looked out of her balcony's sliding glass doors to where the sun would soon set. A wave of happiness and warmth came over her as soon as she noticed it was Tony who had texted. *From my hotel room. It's not out in nature or anything special, but there are less bugs. Where are you watching the sunset from?*

Watching it from the art gallery. Photos with the sunset make for beautiful photos even when they are taken from inside a building, especially when art happens to be in the background. It's quiet here, just me and the security guards.

So, you are also away from the bugs tonight. The quiet isn't as great as the lack of bugs, I kind of miss the noises of the outdoors. Wind blowing on the leaves, animals rustling nearby, that kind of thing. Natala texted back. She set down her hot chocolate and pulled a chair over to the door, then sat down to watch the sunset. Peace had washed over her now, she felt almost at home here in her hotel room. She'd wash her face after the sun set, right now she didn't want to miss out. Nor, she had to admit, did she want to stop texting Tony.

The noises of nature, I miss them. One of my favorite things about shooting outdoors. How was your Vespa tour?

It was an amazing way to see the city. The leaning tower looked much cooler in person than it does in the photographs. Natala clicked send, then her eyes widened. "He's a photographer." She whispered in realization. *That was not meant as an insult,* she quickly texted.

No harm. I understand that. One of the reasons I take photos is to give people a small idea of how beautiful the world is. Then it may inspire someone to go see it for themselves, as you have.

Natala smiled and took another sip of her hot chocolate, looking up to see if the sunset had begun. *I was disappointed that the Vespa was yellow, I'd always imagined that a Vespa was red.*

Did you ask if they had any red Vespas? Your roommate must have chosen the wrong company for your tour.

I should ask her if she did any research about the color of the Vespas, Natala texted back as she laughed. She smiled as the sky began to turn purple. Slowly, she leaned back into the comfy chair and relaxed as she watched the sunset, texting Tony as often as he texted her.

Chapter 7

"Where am I?" Natala blinked and looked out a door, not sure what time it was. "I'm in Italy, in my hotel room." She reminded herself, then noticed the phone on her lap. She picked it up and glanced at the time - 5,00. She'd forgotten where she was more mornings than not, what did that say about her? That she wasn't used to being away from home maybe?

"It's early." She glanced outside at the still dark skies, remembering she'd been texting Tony and watching the sunset last night. Her mug of hot chocolate was set on the floor beside her chair, empty. The hot chocolate must have been a powerful elixir, usually Natala had a hard time falling asleep.

Or maybe it had been something else. Natala thought as she looked at the phone in her hand. She'd enjoyed texting Tony, watching the sunset together even though they were apart. Something about texting him, talking to him, made her feel something... she didn't know how to describe. Warm maybe? Happy? It had been awhile since she had felt this light and peaceful.

Natala stood up and made her way to the bathroom to get ready for the day. And, she realized now, get unready from yesterday. She'd fallen asleep before removing her makeup, washing her face, and brushing her teeth.

As she got closer to the wall that separated her room from Elena's. Natala paused. *Is someone talking to Elena?* She thought. She could hear something coming from the room, and it sounded like voices.

Natala walked over to the door that separated the rooms and put her ear to it, trying to figure out what she'd heard. There were two distinct voices, one was Elena's and the other she couldn't quite recognize. *Why did Elena have someone in her room? Who was it? Was Elena in trouble?* Natala frowned as she listened.

"I can't do this, I just can't. I hate it all so much." Elena said, it sounded like she was crying.

"You're going to get yourself killed Elena Marie Calo. Killed. Then who will I have left?" The mystery voice sounded angry, and must be further away from the wall than Elena was because his voice was harder to make out.

"You say that you love me but you don't show it. You seem to have forgotten who we were. Don't you remember who we used to be? We were younger, I get that. Growing up didn't give you permission to do what you did." Elena's voice was getting louder now, and Natala didn't have to have her ear as close to the door.

"It used to be us against the world. You and me, together. And now what do we have? You left me, went to conquer the world and just left me. Now look where we are. This isn't my fault." Elena's words were followed by the sound of a thump as something hit the wall.

"I love you. I have always loved you and I always will..." The man's voice got softer after that and Natala couldn't hear anything else. She stepped away from the door and looked around her room. The earlier feelings of peace and happiness were gone now.

There was a heaviness in her chest, a worry that was there. Something was off with Elena, she knew that. The longer she'd known the girl, the more evident that had become. But she wasn't sure what, the girl lived with a family as their nanny for goodness' sake. From the sounds of the beginning of their trip, she watched the kids most moments. It didn't seem like there would be much time for her to get into trouble. So, none of this made any sense.

Natala bit her lip as she opened her suitcase and pulled out an outfit to wear for the day. "I'm the one reading too far into things. She's a nanny, not a slave. I'm sure she has a personal life. If she wants to dye her hair, why am I judging her?" She started to remove her makeup, still talking to herself.

"Maybe the disappearing thing is a little weird, but she could have been testing my sense of direction or something. Maybe she thought she was nannying again and saw one of her kids, something ridiculous that makes perfect sense."

She took a quick shower, then brushed out her hair so it was bouncy and ready to go for the day. She kept catching herself looking over at the wall she and Elena shared, wondering what was happening over there. She hadn't heard anything more; Elena must have calmed down. The girl did seem to have two completely different moods, almost two different personalities, and Natala wasn't sure anymore which one was the real Elena. Maybe they both were.

She glanced at her watch. There were still three hours until it was time to meet Elena, and her plan was to go find a bar and get her own breakfast today. Natala loved having a tour guide and not having to worry about getting lost, but by now she felt like she had to try finding her way on her own. The real tourist experience, exploring the area. Embracing some of the spontaneity that Kate had encouraged. Maybe she'd see Tony as she explored.

"Let's see." Natala checked her pockets to make sure she had all she needed, then grabbed her water bottle and headed out of the hotel. "I should try to be more adventurous with my pastry today." She said aloud as she walked down the hotel stairway. "I always have a chocolate croissant, and they are one of the best things I've had in this country. But I should be trying more while I'm here."

She looked around the streets and noted they were fairly empty. She smiled as the sun hit her, feeling the warmth like it was a warm blanket. It had come out while she was showering, a pleasant and beautiful gift.

Natala breathed in a deep breath of fresh air and decided to turn right. She walked down the street until she found a bar. "Hello." She greeted the barista. "I'll take a coffee, and some kind of pastry. What do you recommend?"

"The Sfogliatella is a favorite of visitors, it is delicious." The barista pulled a ruffled looking pastry out of the display and set it down in front of her. "It is a buttery croissant-like pastry filled with custard and orange peel flakes."

Natala smiled. "It looks delicious, I'll take it." She replied, then decided to pay the extra money to sit down with her breakfast. That was an American thing she didn't want to change, eating on the go wasn't her favorite thing. She enjoyed her food a lot more when she sat down and had time to savor all the flavors.

She finished her coffee first, thankful for her water bottle. At home, coffee was something she drank as she ate her breakfast. Here there just wasn't much to espresso, it was a shot. It couldn't last her entire breakfast.

Natala picked up the pastry and examined it a bit closer. She could see the custard coming out between the folds of the pastry, dotted with orange that must be the flakes and peel. "I hope you taste half as good as you look." She said quietly to the pastry, then took a bite.

The flavors danced across her tongue, starting with the buttery taste of the pastry. The rich taste of the thick creamy custard followed, the orange peel accenting the flavor of the custard. Natala couldn't hold back her sigh of happiness after she finished her bite. The custard was the best part.

Natala took a quick photograph of her pastry on her phone and texted it to Kate, telling her that she was having a great trip but looking forward to seeing her soon. Then she took another bite of her pastry as she opened a book on her phone and began to read.

***

"What are you more excited for today, to climb the tower or visit the botanical garden?" Elena asked her as soon as she hopped off the elevator.

Natala, who had just walked into the hotel lobby, blinked. "Good morning to you too. More excited for? I don't think I could pick, both sound really cool. I can't wait to see the view from the top of the tower and all the plants in the garden will be beautiful." She took a sip of her water. "What about you? Which are you more excited for?"

"The tower." Elena giggled. "I'm probably not going to be your favorite person at the garden, I usually just do a quick walk through the place. I prefer to see plants as I'm everywhere else, not go to a place specifically for plants."

Natala shrugged. "Well, today you can tour it for real. I want to spend ten minutes just looking at each plant and tree that we are able to find." She said, trying to keep her tone serious. "Especially bamboo, I heard they have bamboo in the garden. I've never seen bamboo before. I may even have to spend a half hour there."

Elena's eyes widened as she slowed down. "What? That's a really long time."

Natala bent over laughing. "I'm kidding Elena. There is no way I could spend that long just staring at a plant. But it was funny, you have to admit."

Elena sighed before she joined Natala's laughter. "Yeah, funny. Come on, we have a tower to get to."

After the girls climbed the tower and marveled at the view, they made their way to the botanical gardens. "The first university botanical garden in the world?" Natala read from the brochure she'd gotten. "That's pretty impressive."

Elena shrugged. "I guess." She looked at the same brochure, not as interested as Natala was. "There are flowers on the brochure, I don't see any flowers yet. We should go into one of the greenhouses."

"I always think first carries a claim to fame. I don't know how many university botanical gardens in the world there are now, but of all of them this was the first." Natala ignored Elena's complaints and walked into the first greenhouse. "Are those banana trees?" She asked as she looked at the trees.

"They are," Elena replied as he inspected the brochure. "It says this whole greenhouse is banana trees. Look at all of them, that must be like a million bananas." She read from the brochure again. "It's the oldest greenhouse in the garden."

"How old is that?" Natala asked as she looked at the walls. "It seems to still be in good condition. I mean I guess I have no clue what wear and tear happens to greenhouses though."

"It doesn't say how old, but that it is the oldest. Natala, there are succulents in the next greenhouse." Elena exclaimed. "We have to go over there, I love succulents." She walked away quickly, and Natala found herself practically running after her to catch up.

"Wow." She breathed as she looked around the succulent greenhouse. "I've never seen this many succulents before. Not even in pictures, I didn't know this many kinds existed."

"Two hundred species." Elena read. "This is so cool. That one is purple; I've only seen them in pictures. The green ones are the most common, which is probably why there are so many green ones here." She glanced over at Natala. "Do you have any succulents?"

Natala shook her head as she began to walk slowly around the greenhouse, looking at all the species of succulents. "I'm not really a keep plants alive type of person." She replied. "I'm busy I guess; I can't remember to water them."

"Succulents are the best kind of plants for that. I'm leaving mine for a week and they will be perfectly happy when I return without having any water." Elena grinned. "I have six different species, but that doesn't seem like very many right now."

Natala laughed. "I've killed a succulent before. They can only go so long without water, and I never remembered to water them. My roommate has a plant of some type in her room that she keeps alive, but other than that we don't have any plants in our apartment."

"Fancy seeing you two here"

Natala felt a smile come to her face when she spotted Tony. "Hello." She greeted, trying to ignore the feeling in her stomach that came when she saw him.

"Hello." He smiled at her. "Enjoying the garden?"

"Haven't seen too much of it yet, but so far it's beautiful. I've seen more succulents than I knew existed." Natala looked over at Elena, who was inspecting the succulents. "Have you finished photographing the art gallery?"

Tony nodded. "All photos are present and accounted for. I still have some editing to do before they are completely finished, but I thought I'd stop by here first. The plants are always beautiful to see."

"They are." Natala agreed as she looked around the greenhouse at the succulents again. "I didn't realize how much learning could be done here, but each plant has a name and a scientific name and everything."

Tony chuckled. "You could get a whole plant education here." He agreed. "If learning about plants is of utmost interest to you."

Natala shrugged. "I don't know that I want to learn about them that much. I just like seeing them, which is probably why Kate told me to come here in my plans." She glanced over to Elena, who was now crouched down on the floor so she could be eye-level with a succulent. "Elena, are we ready to move on to a different greenhouse?"

"Sure. This is one of the species I have, I was just inspecting it." Elena stood up and walked over to them. "What's next?" She asked.

"I thought keeping track of that was your job." Natala laughed as she he looked at the pamphlet. "The Victoria greenhouse."

She looked up, realizing Elena was halfway out of the greenhouse already. "Elena? You didn't say we were running." She and Tony both followed Elena out, Natala walking and Tony running.

Natala found herself looking around greenhouses and gardens both for the plants, and for any trace of Elena. There were so many different areas and plants to see, she wasn't sure where the younger girl had gone or how she'd gotten away so fast. She hadn't seen Tony since he took off after Elena either.

"Are all these plants edible?" She heard a woman say. Natala looked around the garden, realizing she was in the wild plants area of the botanical garden. "Wow." She whispered. There were many plants here, there were a lot of edible plants. She was getting distracted from looking for Elena now, she needed to get back on track. She blinked and looked away from the plants, trying to decide which way to go next.

"Elena, you are okay." She heard a voice, and frowned. *That sounds like the person who was in Elena's room this morning.* She thought to herself.

"Elena, you're safe. I've got you; you are safe I promise."

Natala walked around the corner and felt her heart drop out of her chest. Elena was there alright, and she wasn't alone. Tony was holding her tightly. "Elena, breathe." Tony said, and Natala couldn't hold back her gasp. That was the voice she'd heard this morning; it was Tony's voice but he had a heavy Italian accent. Tony had been the one in Elena's room that morning?

Tony turned to look at her and she could see that tears were streaming down Elena's face. Natala couldn't think, there were no thoughts going through her brain. Wordlessly, she turned away and ran the other direction. She'd held back from running earlier because she hadn't wanted to cause a scene but she didn't care any longer.

Once Natala got out of the botanical garden, she felt like she could breathe again. She walked down a side road that was just crowded enough she could blend into the crowds perfectly, then began to walk instead of run.

What had just happened? She found herself thinking. *She and Tony had been texting last night, but he'd been in Elena's room? Had he been making everything up and just sitting in the room beside hers? What kind of game had the two been playing with her?*

"Honey, are you okay?" An elderly lady asked her as she walked past.

"I'm fine, thank you." Natala replied, her voice cracking as she spoke. She lifted her hand to her cheek and was supposed to find it was wet, that she had been crying. No wonder this lady was worried about her, she probably made quite a sight.

"Are you sure? Is there someone I can call for you, a husband perhaps?" The lady asked as she looked Natala in the eye.

Natala gave her a small smile. "I will really be fine, thank you for your kindness. I'm just going back to my hotel."

"Be safe dear. And you are in a magical place, tears aren't needed here. You control your adventure."

Natala smiled again at the lady, then walked past her. She wiped her tears away as she talked and took a careful sip of water from her water bottle, trying to calm herself down. Italy didn't feel very magical right now.

"Breathe Natala, breathe." she whispered to herself as she took another sip of water.

Without realizing it, Natala had made her way to the hotel. She blinked for a moment, unsure how that had happened. She had just been trying to get away from the gardens. She walked up the stairs and ran into her room, then started to gather her belongings.

It was only a few minutes later Natala checked out of her hotel room, despite the protests of the front desk clerk and reminders that her reservation for tonight wouldn't be reimbursed. Natala didn't care if it cost her more, she wanted to get away.

As she walked to the nearest bus stop, Natala pulled out her phone and called Kate.

"Well good morning to you." Kate laughed. "I was just getting ready to go to work. How is your adventure?"

"I'm done." Natala's voice broke and she tried to stop herself from crying again.

"Natala?" Kate asked, sounding concerned. "Natala, what happened? Are you okay? Did you get mugged, were you in an accident?"

Natala almost laughed as Kate came up with more and more complicated scenarios. "No, no it's not that. I just..." She sighed and wished she had a free hand to wipe the tears off her cheeks. "I need to come home Kate. Can you get me the earliest flight possible? I'm catching the train to Rome right now."

Kate was quiet for a moment, Natala thought she could hear typing in the background. "There aren't any flights without a layover before the one you already have a ticket for tomorrow. Are you sure you can't wait until then?" She asked gently.

"Give me a layover, I don't care. I just want to be home already." Natala said as she entered the train station.

"Okay, there's a flight in five hours. From Rome to Florida, then Florida to Chicago. It's a two-hour layover, so you'll be stuck at the airport for a while. Will that work for you?" Kate asked her.

Natala shifted her phone to her other hand as she stamped her train ticket. She was glad they were flexible on dates at least; she could use the one that had been planned for her to use tomorrow. "That's fine. It's America, being back in America at least sounds wonderful." She looked around the train station and cringed as she thought about how that sounded to everyone around.

"Okay. I'm booking the tickets; they will be emailed to you so you will have them on your phone. I don't know how long the email will take to get to you but I'm sure they will be there by the time you get to Rome." Kate was quiet for a moment.

Natala found her way to the train and sat down on a bench to wait, keeping her belongings close to her. She looked at the brochure from the museum that was sticking out of her backpack. "I didn't even get to see the bamboo." She whispered sadly.

"Natala?" Kate asked her softly.

"Yes?" Natala asked, squeezing her backpack strap in an attempt to control her emotions better. She just wanted to get home, once she was home everything would be better. This entire trip could just seem like a dream, she could get back to her normal life and forget all of it.

"Do you want me to pick you up at the airport?"

Natala felt the tears spring back to her eyes again. "Yes please." She whispered. "Thank you, Kate."

Chapter 8

In the locker room at work, Natala carefully pulled her ponytail holder out of her hair, trying not to pull it. She used her hands to shake her hair around and let it settle back where it wanted to. "It's always so weird on the first day back." She told one of her coworkers, who had just arrived at work and was getting ready for her shift.

"After two weeks of not even thinking about it? So weird. Two weeks of not having to worry about getting called or working on my day off either." Mandy replied as she began pulling her hair into a bun. "It's like a second Christmas."

Natala laughed as she pulled her purse out of her locker. "Even better than Christmas, because there's no snow."

"Snow isn't your favorite part of the year? You grew up in Wisconsin, isn't it like second nature?" Mandy asked.

"It just means I have plenty of horror stories to tell. Like the time we got two feet of snow but we still had to go to school." Natala watched horror cross Mandy's face, reminding her the girl had grown up in Florida.

"Have a great first day back." Natala called to Mandy as she left the locker room. She made her way out of the building and smiled as the warm sun hit her face. She'd been home for a week now. She hadn't said a word about her time in Italy, making Kate very frustrated.

Natala wasn't sure what she could say, there wasn't a part of her trip she could talk about without saying Tony or Elena's name and she didn't want to think about either of them. There was too much confusion, sadness, and frustration attached to that.

Her phone buzzed, and she pulled it out of her pocket. An email in response to her job application, asking her when she would be able to do an interview.

"Over the phone or in person?" She asked aloud. She could do it a lot sooner over the phone, but did suggesting that make her seem like a problem?

"In person beats over the phone any day."

Natala's head snapped up from her phone and her eyes widened in shock. "What are you doing here?" She asked Tony, looking around the parking lot to see who else was around. She wasn't sure if she was looking for coworkers or checking to see if Elena was with him.

"You owe me a sunset." Tony told her as he put his hands in his pockets.

Natala slipped her phone into her purse and frowned. "What?" She asked, unsure what he was talking about. Unsure why, after everything, she still felt a zing of attraction every time she looked at him.

"A sunset. You agreed to watch the sunset with me, but then you disappeared. They said you checked out of the hotel and left with your luggage." Tony explained. "So, you still owe me a sunset."

"You can go watch a sunset with Elena." Natala told him as she began to walk to her car.

Tony followed her. "Elena?" He asked, his eyebrows furrowed.

"Twenty-two, five foot something, newly blond?" Natala didn't look at him as she pulled her keys out of her purse. "You were in her hotel room in the morning, embracing her in the afternoon."

"That's why you left?" Tony sounded shocked and Natala turned to look at him, trying to gauge his reaction. He did truly look shocked; did he think he could just play innocent? Try to convince her she hadn't seen what she had seen?

"I left twenty-four hours earlier than I planned; it wasn't that much of a change. I missed my country and figured I'd give you and Elena some space." Natala opened her car door and leaned against it.

"Natala, Elena is my sister." Tony told her.

Natala blinked as that registered. "Your sister?" She frowned. "She lives in Italy."

"Yes, she lives in Italy. That's where I was born, my parents were both from there. When my mom was pregnant with Elena, she and I immigrated to America. Elena and I spent summers in Italy when we were old enough to fly by ourselves, our father never left the country. When Elena needed to get away from someone, she thought Italy was the perfect opportunity. She was already in love with the country." Tony explained.

Natala was quiet as many thoughts came to her mind. If Elena needed to get away from someone, maybe that's why she'd been so jumpy sometimes. That might also explain why Tony had an Italian accent when he wanted to, if he'd spent more time in Italy than he had let on when she'd met him.

"Is that why Elena dyed her hair?" She voiced the first of her thoughts aloud.

"Yes. The man she is trying to get away from, she saw in Italy. But that is her story to tell." Tony watched Natala carefully.

Natala wasn't sure what to think. Had she been hasty for not asking questions instead of leaving? Some things suddenly made sense, like why Elena had given Tony her phone number. And how Tony had always seemed to pop up exactly where she and Elena were. Why had Tony come here? She'd told him where he worked, so had he come to find her? And how did she feel about that?

"Why didn't you tell me?" She asked. "When you first introduced Elena, why didn't you say she was your sister?"

Tony shrugged and shifted from one foot to another. "I don't know." He replied. "It wasn't really a conscious decision. I didn't realize that I didn't tell you. I'm not with her that much, I don't know that I've ever introduced her to someone. It isn't a habit to say 'Oh this is Elena, she is my sister.'"

Natala glanced down at her purse when her phone buzzed. It was most likely Kate, wondering where she was. "I have to go."

"Watch one more sunset with me?" Tony asked her. "Tonight, anywhere you'd like to watch it from."

As much as she wanted to stop it, Natala felt a smile come to her face. She'd tried not to fall for this man, she'd thought he had broken her trust. But something in her still felt drawn to him, felt more complete when she was around the man. "Okay." She said softly, naming a local park. "I'll meet you there at 8. Sunset is a bit after that."

"I'll look forward to it." Tony said as Natala got into her car. She put her key into the ignition and buckled her seatbelt before pulling out of her parking spot. Her phone buzzed again, reminding her that she hadn't checked it to see what Kate had said. Or to make sure it was actually Kate. "Oh well."

Ten minutes later, Natala walked into the apartment. She sighed happily as she noticed the air smelled like pot roast. "It smells so good in here."

"Thanks." Kate replied as she eyed Natala curiously. "Have you heard back about any of your applications?"

Natala grinned. "I did, one of them wants to schedule an interview. I'm not sure if it can be done by phone, so I'll have to ask that." She bit her lip as she set her purse on a chair. "I just don't want to take too many days off to go to an interview when maybe I'll stay."

Kate laughed as she opened a cupboard and pulled some plates out of it. "Come on Natala, you aren't going to stick around. I'm not looking forward to losing you as a roommate, but we both know you want to be back home. Personally, I'm surprised it didn't happen sooner. You moved here for him. Your job isn't anything special, it makes sense to be back in Wisconsin."

Natala shrugged. "I'll still have to find a good job, something comparable. Do we still have gelato for dessert?"

Kate opened the freezer door, revealing three different bowls of gelato. "No, none at all." She said with a giggle. "The problem is that now you've gotten me obsessed with gelato and once you leave, I'll have to buy it for myself."

***

Natala pulled her sweatshirt closer as she walked to the park. It might be May, but it was none too warm in the Midwest. She looked at the sky, glad the sunset hadn't started yet. Tony couldn't protest that she'd shorted him a sunset.

She walked into the park, and over to her favorite bench. This particular park was one of her favorites because there was no playground, just lots of flowers. It was usually quieter than any other park because there weren't any children running around.

"Good evening." Tony walked over to her.

Natala looked up and smiled when she noticed the flowers he was carrying. "What are those?" She asked.

"Apology flowers." Tony replied, then paused and looked at the flowers. "Well, they are really just flowers; but they come with an apology." He handed Natala the flowers.

Natala smiled again and took the bouquet. She recognized the pink roses and the white orchids, but wasn't sure what all the other flowers were.

"I never meant to mislead you about who Elena is, I really never thought about it. I apologize for not telling you she was my sister."

"Apology accepted." Natala replied as she held the flowers, silently thinking that she'd never gotten flowers from someone unrelated to her before. Her ex had never been one for gifts or gestures.

Tony sat down beside her on the bench. "Truth is, I enjoyed meeting you on the plane. That's why I found you outside the pasta class you'd told me about and took you to watch the sunset. When you seemed lost in the city, I thought Elena would be the perfect answer. And I'll admit, I liked the idea of being able to see you again too." He explained. "Being able to keep track of you, in a not-meant-to-be-creepy way."

Natala looked at the sky, noting a tinge of orange starting to come across it. "I enjoyed watching the sunsets with you in Italy." She admitted. "I enjoyed the country, and I had gotten to know Elena and like her too. But she always seemed to be hiding something or hiding from something. When I saw you two together and realized you were the one, I'd heard in her hotel room that morning it seemed like everything made sense." Natala shrugged. "And I realized what was important as I explored Italy. I saw all the family-owned shops and realized Elena reminded me of how my sister used to be. So, I came back a day early."

"Tell me about your family." Tony encouraged as he leaned against the back of the bench and looked into the sky.

"My parents have been married twenty-seven years now, my mom does private accounting for like three different companies. My dad is an auto mechanic and auto instructor, I guess, as he is the one all the newbies train under." Natala smiled. "We've heard plenty of funny stories from his experiences. And I have a younger sister and younger brother, they are twins." She glanced at Tony. "What about you? Do you have siblings other than Elena?"

"It's just Elena and I," Tony replied. "I don't hear from her all that much because she's in Italy and I'm not there all the time."

"I'm moving back home, to Wisconsin, to be closer to my family." Natala ran a strand of hair through her hands. "Just, you know, to put everything out on the table."

Tony looked at her instead of the setting sun now, making Natala nervous. Nervous in a way she couldn't quite explain, like this was an important moment in her life and she wasn't sure how it would go. "I like you, Natala. If we are putting everything on the table then I'll add that to it. I can't explain exactly why, but something about your spirit draws me to you and I haven't been able to stop thinking about you since I met you on that plane."

Natala felt her cheeks heat up. "I don't exactly know what to say to that." She replied, her voice shaky.

"That ex of yours really dropped the ball. You don't seem used to receiving compliments." Tony reached out and put a strand of Natala's hair behind her ear. "You seem like an amazing woman Natala. I admire your free-spirit to go on a vacation to another country by yourself. I love watching you get excited by all the little things in Italy like the palm trees." He glanced down at the flowers that were now in Natala's lap, "and the things here like flowers. I admire how hard-working you are and how you don't seem to let anything stop you from doing what you want. I'd like to get to know you more, take you out on dates and watch countless sunsets with you anywhere in America or around the world."

Natala found herself having trouble breathing after that speech. No one had ever said anything like that to her, no one had ever told her she was hard-working or that she had a free-spirit. "I'm attracted to you in a way I've never been attracted to anyone before." She admitted softly, looking down at her flowers. "You travel the entire world for a living and take beautiful photos of all kinds of beautiful things, I don't see how someone like you can be attracted to someone like me."

Tony looked into her eyes, then put his hand on her cheek and leaned in to kiss her. In that moment - with the sunset as a colorful backdrop - Natala knew what it was like to feel sparks.

Also by Kimberly R. Rose

Luna Family Trilogy
Italian Sunsets
Italian Sunsets

About the Author

An early childhood educator turned small business woman and author; Kimberly R. Rose grew up in a small town in Wisconsin. She has loved reading since she was a child, often neglecting her schoolwork to read a book. That love for reading turned into inspiration for writing. Her favorite things in life are her faith, her family, and chocolate.

Italian Sunsets is Kimberly's debut novella, the first in the Luna Family Trilogy.